This copy of

A FOAL FOR CANDY
by Diana Pullein-Thompson

belongs to

_____

_____

Diana Pullein-Thompson

A
Foal for
Candy

SPARROW
BOOKS

A Sparrow Book
Published by Arrow Books Limited
17–21 Conway Street, London W1P 5HL

An imprint of the Hutchinson Publishing Group

London Melbourne Sydney Auckland
Johannesburg and agencies
throughout the world

First published 1981
© Diana Pullein-Thompson 1981

Set in Linoterm Baskerville
by Book Economy Services, Cuckfield, Sussex

Made and printed in Great Britain
by the Anchor Press Ltd
Tiptree, Essex

ISBN 0 09 927240 7

1

It was the summer term when we stood in a rented field looking at our cream mare, Candy. She had been desperately ill earlier in the year, making us aware how sorely we needed more than the two looseboxes owned by our parents.

'She certainly is very fat,' admitted my elder sister, Briony, 'but then look at the grass, hock-deep and green as a billiard table. She's bound to put on weight here.'

'Her belly is big,' I said, 'but the rest of her is thin. Her poor neck is like an ironing board.'

I put out a hand which Candy licked before sniffing my hair, as though it were hay which she might sample if the scent were right. Having nursed her for several weeks through two different afflictions I felt a special affection for her. We were bound together by a mutual struggle to keep her alive.

'You always were over-anxious about her, Lynne, like a mother with a delicate child. You watch for trouble.'

'All the same, Briony,' I said, 'perhaps next time we have the vet. . . ? Isn't it just possible that she may be in foal?'

'I do hope not.'

'You'll get two for the price of one. Isn't that a bonus?' suggested my brother David. 'I should have thought any horse dealer would be delighted in the circumstances.'

A frown wrinkled Briony's forehead as she kicked the

turf. She saw herself as an agent, seeking to match ponies and their owners so well that both would be content. Dealers, she thought, existed mainly to make money, whereas she aimed to provide a service. Money was secondary, but, of course, important if she were going to pay for the stabling she hoped to find to rent until she could afford to put up five or six looseboxes in the bit of unused garden behind our house.

'Depends on the foal, doesn't it?' she replied at last. 'A mare who has been ill and dosed with drugs can't be expected to produce a winner. It's very hard to tell with ponies anyway – some don't get very big until the end of their time.'

As Briony spoke I put my arm over Candy's neck.

'If only you could speak,' I declared as thousands had before me, 'how easy life would be. Tell us how you feel, show us . . . but there, look, didn't something kick in her stomach? Did you see?'

'Imagination,' said David with his usual scepticism. 'You can see almost anything if you want to badly enough.'

'But I don't want Candy to have a foal,' I objected. 'I want to ride her in the summer holidays – you know that.'

'No one's buying foals just now because money is so short,' said Briony, continuing her gloomy line of thought. 'All right, Lynne, you win. Next time the vet comes I'll ask her to have a look, but do remember that ponies always blow themselves out when they get into a field of lush grass. There's nothing abnormal about that. Too much can be as bad as too little. I wouldn't dare put a little one in here for fear he developed laminitis. If your suspicions are well founded we'll have to look around for another foal to keep Candy company. Two winter better than one alone.'

'Start a sort of stud farm – great!' said David. 'But it

wouldn't make any money.'

'No, certainly not a stud farm, because we haven't bred this one and we don't know who its father is – if there is one. He could be an Irish carthorse, and nobody in England buys carthorses these days unless they're pedigree Shires. Shaun Lester is terrible – you remember the man I bought her from – I mean it's bad enough selling me a pony with strangles, but if there's to be a foal, well, that's pretty diabolical.'

'I don't suppose he knew,' David said.

'But think of Candy,' I urged my brother and sister. 'She's only just four and think how much she's been through, poor thing. She isn't even fully grown yet.'

'Now we're all counting our chickens before they're hatched. Come on, there's a lot to be done. Back to work,' said Briony. 'A girl of eighteeen is coming to see me in ten minutes. She's just started work as a secretary and she wants to fulfil a lifelong ambition and have a pony of her own. It's got to be a docile animal who won't hot up when only ridden at weekends. I was thinking this morning that Candy might fit the bill.'

'Oh, no!' I cried at once, suddenly seeing a future I had planned disappearing from under my feet like a landslide. 'I know dealing is your business, but you promised, you promised most faithfully that I could school her and keep her through the summer. You said . . .'

'All right, all right, don't fly off the handle! It was just a vague idea, no more. It's important that Candy should find a kind and suitable home eventually. She's docile and kind and possibly not very strong because of the illness. Weekend riding might be a good answer for her if she has a weakened constitution.'

'She's special,' I insisted. 'Can't you see that? She prefers human beings to other ponies. Look how she's standing with us now as though she's one of us.'

'She probably belonged to Irish tinkers, and lived tethered among the caravans, dogs and children. I expect they fed her scraps from the fireside. She has that look about her,' Briony told us. 'Shaun Lester works through a dealer in Ireland, a man who roams the countryside with a truck making offers for any passable animal he sees anywhere. After trying them under the saddle and giving them a pretty primitive check for soundness, he ships them off to this country with a three-month warranty. Half the time Shaun Lester has no idea from whom his purchases were originally bought. He just trusts his Irish contact's judgement and insists that he'll send back any pony that isn't sound or rideable.'

Now we left Candy standing at the gate and wandered down the lane to home. The shadows were lengthening, birds were singing their last songs and in someone's garden tobacco plants opened their petals to scent the air, catching the evening rays of a sun which had blazed all day with tropical splendour. Fred, the local horse expert, was standing by our yard, a long staff in his weatherbeaten right hand. A frown like a plough's furrow lay across his leathery face, which was indeed the colour of freshly turned clay soil, and his blue eyes wore their habitual irritated expression. A groom for many years, he was now a horse-mad man without a horse.

'I reckon that cream mare's in foal. She's not interested in other horses when she should be, not even in the string from the racing stables when they go by. She's got a belly on her too.' As Fred spoke he looked Briony up and down as though she had some drawback and was herself a pony who needed a trim, new shoes, a tail pulled or something. He was, we thought, jealous of my sister because she had so many ponies passing through her hands and he had none. She was doing what he would have liked to do, only he had never had enough money to set up on his own. I could understand his feelings a little because I was equally envious of our neighbour, Mirabelle, who had two gorgeous ponies of her own and the company of her parents' labrador dog.

There was the additional irritation of Briony's fame, for she had been astonishingly successful in both show-jumping and three-day events before Talisman, her cross-country horse, had died and The Mountain, her jumper, had become incurably lame. It was Talisman's death at the end of a gruelling course which had made her decide to give up competitions and, later, to start her agency, the Pony Seekers. But Fred did not seem to take account of this tragedy. In his view she had been lucky since birth. And now he was irritated by our thoughtful silence.

'Well, what do you say to that? You don't care, it seems,' he called as we turned towards the house.

'We've more or less come to the same conclusion,' David replied crisply.

'A bit late in the day,' scoffed Fred with his loud, scornful laugh which is recognizable from quite a distance. 'She'll be bagging up soon.'

'Thank you for watching her and thank you for your advice,' Briony sounded conciliatory. 'The vet's going to examine her.'

'You don't need the vet. He'll cost you a pretty penny. I'm telling you the truth. Has the vet cured The Mountain yet?'

'Unfortunately not, but then show-jumpers' legs do go sometimes.'

Briony turned into our yard, with its two looseboxes, forage shed and garage.

'I wish someone would find that man a job. He's horribly under-occupied,' remarked David in an undertone. 'He'd love to be part of us, the Pony Seekers, but if he was he'd try to rule us, because he's sure he knows more than Briony about everything.'

Now a little yellow car came buzzing round the corner, driven by a red-haired girl with deep brown eyes.

'My client,' Briony said, 'and luckily she's small – can't be more than eight and a half stone – so a pony will do. I wonder whether she's got a field with a shelter or a stable.'

My sister smiled, her face lighting up as it does when she's happy, her eyes green and bright as the first spring leaves.

2

The vet came ten days later to check a pony for one of Briony's clients. She examined Candy internally and declared that she was in foal, and then we didn't know whether to be happy or sad. Would the foal be all right? The vet wasn't sure. The mare's illnesses had been very debilitating, she told us.

After she had gone, Briony repeated that Candy and her child would need a companion. Our sister had recently made more money than she had expected and, being naturally impetuous, she decided to spend some of it as soon as a sensible opportunity arose.

So, on a bright and windy Saturday afternoon, we found ourselves on a slope in the Cotswolds at a well-known horse fair where the keen breeze was like a welcome splash of cold water on our hot faces.

'Fifty pounds I'm offered, fifty pounds, sixty . . . sixty-five, sixty-five I'm bid. Come on, ladies and gentlemen, a lovely mare, quiet to ride and drive, good with children too, and warranted sound. Seventy-five, thank you, eighty, eighty I'm bid, eighty-five, ninety, ninety-five, one hundred, one hundred, I'm bid.'

I don't like horse sales. I always think they're humiliating for the animals being sold, and I've yet to see a pony looking happy in a sale ring; they seem to know that they're about to face a change in their lives and the old, the sick and the lame seem to be aware that their faults are apparent for all to see. Some of the spectators' comments are cruel. People talk about 'old screws', 'planks', 'ponies only fit for dog meat', and then I wonder how they would like to run round a ring with scores of critical eyes noting their faults. I long to buy the thin and broken-down ponies, take them home and make them fat and well again — above all, show them that someone cares.

We were not in the bidding for the rather scrawny brown gelding being trotted up and down the oval ring by a grey-haired lady in corduroy trousers. Briony was interested in Devon Melody, a registered Dartmoor pony believed in foal to a well-known registered Dartmoor stallion. A red bay with black points, Melody possessed a charming dish face with a shapely white star partially hidden by a thick forelock. She carried little hair on her legs and, despite her sturdiness, had an air of delicacy about her which would suggest even to the ignorant that she was well bred.

'Nowadays pedigree foals are the only ones which sell. People are such snobs,' complained Briony. 'There's absolutely no point in buying an animal without papers.'

Soon the rather pathetic brown was sold to a hatchet-faced man in a cap, and then Melody was led into the ring, described as eleven hands two inches, quiet to ride, six years old, warranted sound and believed in foal . . . etc., etc. . . . Briony waited until there was a pause in the bidding, which started well, before waving her catalogue and shouting 'Eighty-five pounds'. Thereafter she was firmly in the auctioneer's eyes and had only to nod her head to register a bid. Determined to have the mare, she went on until everyone else had stopped, and then the hammer fell and the autioneer asked, 'Name, please?' and because of her past fame heads turned when she replied.

'Don't buy anything else,' David advised. 'You've spent enough for one afternoon. I think we should go home now.'

'Sssh! My eye's on a lovely little roan with a front as long as a table. Ponies are going for a song today. Honestly, I don't know where all the money's gone. I'd be a fool not to take advantage of the situation.'

The light of battle shone in Briony's face, so that I wondered suddenly whether auctions intoxicated her. Would she go on and on like a gambler until all her money was spent? It was a disturbing thought.

'A roan? Which roan?' I asked, feeling that, like Dr Watson questioning Sherlock Holmes, I was perhaps unable to grasp the obvious.

'The gelding backed at three and then turned away. You must have seen me examining him . . . wonderful short cannon bones, strong quarters, wide chest and oceans of heart room. A great pony, Lynne . . . stamina combined with elegance. I bet he moves like a dream.'

'Who for?'

'No one. On spec.'

'But I thought you weren't going to buy anything unless you had a home waiting for it?' I said.

'There are always exceptions to a rule.'

'But Briony,' David cut in, 'you said that the whole point of the Pony Seekers was that you only purchased very carefully for customers who were already looking for a pony. You said you were running an agency, not a dealer's business.'

'True, but David, I must be allowed a little fun occasionally. I've done rather well lately so why shouldn't I have a tiny spending spree? You two can school the roan for me. He's much too good-looking to be in this sale.'

'Oh, I see, it's a rescue operation. Is that it?' asked David cryptically. 'Come on, Lynne, somehow I don't want to watch Briony buying another one.'

We wandered off in search of Melody, who was

rather shy as though she had never been cherished, while Briony paid for her.

'I'm glad our dear sister has parted with some of her money. I hate to think of her walking around with hundreds of pounds in her pockets. It's so easy to be mugged and she's so careless she could easily lose it.'

'You don't seem to trust her very much.'

'Love many, trust a few, learn to paddle your own canoe,' quoted David.

'Mother's dictum,' I said.

'Yes, but a good one. Listen, she's bought the roan. Now we must drag her home. I don't think our parents realize that their eldest daughter is such a worry to us.'

'Oh, David, you exaggerate. I don't worry at all. But for Briony we wouldn't get any riding – just think of that. Here she comes.'

'Enough is enough,' our sister said, standing for a moment with sparkling green eyes in a happy smiling face. 'I've kept my self-control. Home now!'

We fetched the roan and Melody, let down the ramp of the truck and took them up in turn.

'First hurdle over. Both quiet to box. Great!' Briony said. 'Mind you tie them with slip knots – *firm* slip knots.' This done, we shut the ramp and leapt into the cab.

'Nothing for the secretary?' asked David.

'No, two gambles,' Briony said, a smile still hovering on her face.

She started the engine using a bit of choke, put the vehicle into first gear, released the handbrake and drove slowly across the bumpy field to a stony lane which led to the main road.

'I never thought I'd make three good sales in a row,' she reflected, referring to three families for whom she had found suitable mounts very quickly at extremely reasonable prices, leaving her with a good profit. 'Next

14

Saturday I want you both to come with me on a pony hunt. I've got four or five to see.'

'But what about Candy?' I objected. 'She may foal that day. You know the vet said it could be quite soon, even within a fortnight. We must be there in case she needs help.'

'Most ponies manage excellently on their own. They know instinctively what to do; complications are rare. Usually only highly strung thoroughbreds need human assistance.'

'Usually doesn't mean always. And she's not most ponies,' I argued. 'She's different. She's been mortally ill, and she's the sort who always has difficulties with everything. Fred says cream ponies are delicate.'

'Oh, Lynne!' cried Briony in exasperation. 'You over-dramatize everything. Let's wait until next Saturday, then we'll know whether she's bagging up, when the milk begins to move into her udders and she softens underneath.'

'All right. She's your pony, not mine. I just felt . . . Oh, never mind. . . .'

I fell silent, thinking Briony might be right, that perhaps I was being neurotic and silly. The sun was a ball of burning gold in the wide skies of the west. Trees were shaking leaf-laden boughs in a jaunty little breeze which whispered in the tall grasses and sang in the fields of wheat rolling away from us towards the horizon. Briony turned off on to a minor road and here on a hill of rippling corn the truck began to spit, gurgle and grind to a halt.

'Oh, no!' our sister cried, changing to bottom gear. 'Oh, no, I can't bear it! It's going to break down. Oh, that will be the end, right here miles from anywhere! Please, truck, keep going! Come on, you monster, come on!' Her foot was right down on the accelerator and she leaned forwards as though urging a lazy horse to go

15

faster.

'Petrol? Oil?' asked David.

'I checked before I left.'

'Water in the battery? The radiator?'

'Of course. I'm not an imbecile. I'm an adult – in case you've forgotten – and I do know the elementary things.' Briony smiled again as though to soften her words.

'Something serious then. Fan belt, perhaps?' suggested David, trying to sound knowledgeable.

'A mechanical failure! Oh, what a blow! Just when everything was going so well.'

Briony put on the handbrake. 'Damn all motors!'

'Look out! Look at that!' As I shouted I felt my eyes grow large. Grey smoke was rising in gentle spirals before the windscreen.

'Fire!' cried David. 'All out!'

We leapt from the cab as sinister tongues of flame started to lick the bonnet, followed by more smoke billowing into the balmy air.

'The extinguisher!' shouted Briony, leaping back into the cab. 'Get the horses out!'

'The petrol tank may explode!' argued David, bumping into Briony as she reached ground level again. 'Give me that! You're quicker with ponies than I am.'

I was at the back now, undoing the ramp, my heart thumping like a four-pound hammer hitting a sturdy post. Surprisingly, my hands worked mechanically as though they sensed the need for calm efficiency. I went to the roan first because he was pawing the straw, undid the slip knot and backed him down the ramp. Then Briony was untying Melody, saying in a pitiable voice, 'Oh, why does this have to happen to me? Why? Why me?' Melody wouldn't back, but eventually Briony managed to turn her round on the ramp, while the roan was snorting and leaping in the air like a wild mustang,

16

frightened by the hiss of the extinguisher's liquid on the flames, by the smoke and, perhaps most of all, by the stink of burning plastic and rubber.

'Jerk on the halter rope! Speak to him! Don't let him go! Whoa, whoa there! Steady. Walk now, walk.' Briony's voice was suddenly calm, for she knew that it was essential that the ponies should not sense her fear.

'It's all right, nothing to be frightened of. Walk on, walk now, walk.' I started to lead the roan down the road away from the truck. Would Briony ever be able to raise the money to buy another if this one was a write-off? I asked myself. She might, of course, opt for a trailer instead, which would be cheaper to run, but then she would have to buy a strong car, jeep or Land-Rover to pull it. And such an expense would be beyond her.

As the fire subsided a man in a red car drew up and asked whether he could help. When I explained what had happened he made tut-tutting noises.

'Sounds bad, very bad. I don't think there's anything I can do.' His teeth flashed as he glanced at Briony. 'Is that your sister?'

'Yes, she's in charge,' I told him.

The roan was grabbing huge mouthfuls of roadside grass as our would-be rescuer talked to Briony, before following David to inspect the engine.

'There's an awful lot of electrical wiring burnt out. You haven't a hope of getting home in this vehicle. It must have started with a short circuit. Can't help, I'm afraid. I'll stop at the next garage anyway and see if they can help you.'

He sped away and the sun sank a little lower in the sky while we wondered whether he had been able to stir anyone to come and save us, but we knew that most garages closed down on Saturday afternoons, apart from keeping one assistant to sell petrol. Soon Briony got out the map while David held Melody. After study-

17

ing it for a few moments, he announced that we were only ten miles from home.

'That's nothing,' she said. 'I walked ten miles when I was ten.'

'Can't we ride?' asked David, who loathes trudging along roads.

'We only have halters and this roan hasn't been ridden for a year,' mused Briony, 'and Melody is too heavily in foal – it wouldn't be fair to add to the weight she's already carrying. Besides, she's too small for us.'

We waited a little longer in case a mechanic turned up. Then we fastened the ramp, shut down the bonnet, locked up and set off for home.

'At least it isn't raining,' Briony said.

'And we're all sound in wind, limb and eye. Let's look on the bright side,' suggested David with a mocking laugh.

'I'll get someone to come on Monday and put the wretched thing right or tow it home, which will cost a mountain of money,' Briony told us. 'That nice bloke, Tim, might do it one evening after work. He likes to make a spot of money on the side.'

'I'm tired of walking,' David announced after a couple of miles. 'This is ridiculous. I'm going to try the roan. He's been backed, after all.'

'Fair enough,' agreed Briony. 'But, Lynne, if he falls off and hurts himself, will you please tell Mother that he rode this pony against my advice.' As Briony spoke she gave my brother a leg-up. 'I shall lead him. He's not schooled, you see, and you've only got a halter, and a year is quite a while in a pony's life – about the same as three in ours.'

The roan wasn't worried as long as I led the way with Melody, and after a while we began to look to the future.

'No one's answered your advertisement for stabling,

I suppose?' my brother said.

'Not yet. Give them time. I shall shut down in December if I don't have any luck. Sell up almost everything.'

'What do you mean by "almost"?'

'Well, there's The Mountain and then there's room for one other, isn't there? I'm not having sick horses without shelter again.'

'It isn't fair,' I grumbled. 'I wish our parents were rich and could afford to buy us our own ponies. Look at Mirabelle, with two ponies of her own and all those posh clothes.'

'She isn't any happier than you are,' David pointed out, 'because her legs are fat. She would give anything to have your legs and Briony's nose – she told me so.'

'I say, what confidences!' I laughed.

'It isn't funny to be fat,' David reproached me. 'It's rather sad.'

Now the sun lay like a king in crimson robes on the sky's bed and everywhere the birds were singing their lovely evening songs.

'Your turn, Lynne,' David said, jumping off the roan, whom we had decided to call Rocket. 'Come on, up you get!'

And riding with Briony at my mount's head, I felt that special happiness which is aroused in me by a beautiful landscape bathed in the light of a sinking sun. I wanted to sing, but with the truck partly burned out some four miles back, singing wasn't tactful. Briony's slouch suggested gloom. Fate, she felt, was always against her. Every gain she made was almost immediately counteracted by a loss, and her losses were our losses too.

'Surely we could keep a few ponies through the winter in New Zealand rugs if you can't find or afford more stabling?' suggested David. 'I mean, isn't that a possibility we ought to consider?'

'One and The Mountain, that's all.' Briony's tone defied argument.

'Candy and her foal?' I asked cautiously.

'Not necessarily. It depends on what can be sold most easily as winter approaches. Sentiment won't come into it, I'm afraid.'

'Only The Mountain is to be kept for sentiment,' I said, rather unfairly.

'That's different. And it's for me to make the decision when the time comes. So please shut up.'

Dusk came and brought white-scutted rabbits on the banks under the occasional thorn hedges. An owl in an ash tree looked down on us with huge eyes ringed with pale circles. Our stomachs grumbled, wanting food, and our thoughts turned grey as the darkening sky. We stopped at a phone box to let our parents know that we were delayed, but they were out.

'Someone invited them to drinks – I remember now,' Briony said.

'Should we ring Mirabelle and ask her to check Candy?' I asked, suddenly anxious.

'No, no, do keep your sense of proportion. I just hope that truck won't ruin me – labour costs so much these days,' complained Briony. Then a cat sprang from a wall and Rocket leapt high in the air and turned tail. I grabbed the top of the halter, while David hung on to its rope. Hanging on to the mane I pulled myself straight, for I had slipped to one side.

'Whoa! Steady, walk.' We calmed him down.

'"Backed and then turned away" could mean anything,' David said.

'Or nothing,' I added.

'It's an accepted term,' Briony told us. 'It means he has been mounted and is quiet when someone is on his back. I've bought him for his splendid conformation.'

At last we came to our fields and there was Briony's lame show jumper The Mountain, who had once won so many prizes for her, big and dark and beautiful with rippling muscles and wise, graceful head and a look of calm experience in his eyes. And Mirabelle, our plump, rich friend, was pedalling her new bicycle, her red hair bright in the gathering dusk.

'Hullo, new ponies! What a dear little mare. Is she Dartmoor?' Mirabelle dismounted, her freckled face breaking into a smile. I looked at her well-rounded legs. Did they really make so much difference to her?

'We've walked ten miles. We're tired,' David said. 'The truck went on fire.'

'Flames everywhere,' I said, wanting to conjure up a picture.

'Oh, bad luck! cried Mirabelle. 'You need a new one. Yours is going rusty anyway. My dad changes cars every year. He likes to have the newest model. If you drive such a tatty old thing everyone thinks your business is about to collapse. Your truck is your shop front.'

We all turned away of one accord, wondering whether our wretched neighbour would ever learn tact. Worse still, there was Fred, walking up the road towards the pub, wearing a hacking jacket with a rose in its buttonhole.

'More new ones? Been to the fair? Where's the truck? Broken down? Girls never know how to look after motors! That bay's in foal, isn't she? Hasn't long to go. Going in for breeding now, are you? Not much money in that these days except with chasers or racehorses.'

'The cream mare's foal will need a companion,' explained Briony, resting a hand on Melody's neck.

'But it's not arrived yet. Could be born dead. You musn't count your chickens before they're hatched. Who's the sire of this one, then?' Fred pointed at Melody's belly.

21

'A very famous Dartmoor stallion,' Briony told him coldly, angered by his curiosity. 'We're not utterly foolish. And the mare has an excellent pedigree. I have it with me.' Briony patted her pocket.

'Now don't take on. I mean well. You've always got to be so careful when you buy at horse fairs. The best ponies don't get taken to that sort of place. Misfits, odds and ends, crib-biters, wind-suckers, the unreliables and the vicious – those make up most of the animals at fairs. But what about the roan? He seems a good sort. Would look fine in a trap, that one would.'

'Been backed and turned away for a year. He's only four. We shall school him on,' said Briony as we all turned into our yard.

'I shall call him Mr Know-all,' Mirabelle said of Fred.

'I think Mr Pain-in-the-neck is better,' David countered.

'I'm terribly afraid that he's a misfit himself,' Briony admitted. 'He means well, just as he said, but tact is not in his list of virtues.'

'And now I'm going to check Candy,' I announced.

I ran and found her grazing happily, her dark eyes full of contentment. She raised her head when she saw me, then cantered up to nuzzle my pockets.

3

Melody and Candy settled down very well together as though they enjoyed each other's company, although Candy would always leave the little bay, preferring to stand with me, if I went to the field.

The day after our long walk home Briony was busy getting the truck towed to a garage, which was quite an achievement on a Sunday, and the next day we were back at school with lots of homework to occupy us in the evening.

Meanwhile Briony lunged Rocket, who turned out to be left-handed – or hoofed – and therefore hated to go round to the right. She had to muster all her skill and experience to force him to do what she wanted. But she was still delighted with his appearance and carriage. He moved, she told us, like a champion, with only one fault – his action was a trifle high. 'But he more than makes up for it in other ways. He holds his tail like an Arab and he seems to go naturally with his hocks under him,' she said.

I visited the two mares every day before I left for school, when I returned and again last thing at night. My care for them was prompted not only by affection, but also by a need to study them, for recently I had become determined to try to be a vet. I began to take a greater interest in physics and chemistry at school – two subjects which I had previously found boring – because I knew that I must pass these at O Level if I were to follow the career I was mapping out for myself. I had already selected Glasgow as my first choice of university because its veterinary college was set in spacious, partly wooded grounds which suggested to me that I might at last be able to own a dog while studying there.

Three days after the fair, Briony asked me whether I would ride Rocket as she was too heavy for any pony under fourteen two and he was only thirteen three hands high. I put away my physics book, fetched my crash cap and stuffed my feet and legs into rubber riding boots.

'I want to sell him fairly quickly,' my sister said, 'because the truck is going to cost me a lot of money.'

We saddled him up together. Briony had lunged him in tack several times and found him quite accustomed to it. 'And I've more or less won the battle to make him go well on the right rein,' she told me. 'Most ponies are either left – or right-handed.'

I mounted Rocket in the school with Briony at his head, and he stood quite still with his ears – a good signpost to a pony's feelings – well relaxed. At first Briony led him round the school, which was actually only an area marked out with old oil cans, and he went well. 'I'm sure he's been more than backed. I get the impression that he's been ridden out a bit,' she said. 'He strides, whereas a newly broken pony wanders.'

I didn't answer, because I was concentrating on my riding, which is never as expert as I want it to be. 'Heels down, chin up, shoulders square,' I was telling myself.

'Shall I let you loose now?' As Briony spoke she let go of the bridle and moved back into the centre of the school, and the minute she had gone I felt Rocket's stride shorten and his ears flash back as his tail swished.

'Use your legs! Go on – squeeze! Kick!' Briony shouted. 'You're losing impulsion.'

I obeyed her at once but Rocket was as unresponsive as a sack of bran. Then he dug his toes in, stopping with calculated suddenness.

'Walk on! Walk on!' I commanded in the authoritative tones Briony had used while he was on the lunge rein.

'Hang on, I'll come to his head again. Perhaps we're taking him too fast. Just a minute.'

But she was too late, for as she spoke he reared up on his hind legs, up and up, and, taken by surprise, I slipped back in the saddle and pulled on the reins to save myself from sliding over his quarters. And then suddenly we were toppling, and the earth was coming up to meet me and fear, quick as lightning, flashed through my mind before I landed with a thud on my back. And then, for one terrible moment, I thought Rocket was coming down on top of me, that I would be squashed like a slug under a gardener's boot. I rolled over and he came down beside me, his legs kicking in all directions. I caught a blow on my left side from one of his hoofs. My head span and stars danced for a second before my eyes. And then Briony was there, with her eyes looking large with concern.

'Are you all right, Lynne?'

'Yes, yes, of course.'

My voice was a little shrill and the field was tipping crazily as my sister's face receded. Rocket scrambled to his feet and shook himself so that his stirrups rattled and, thinking that I should do the same, I held out my hands and Briony took them and pulled. Then the field straightened and fell back into place.

'Huh!'

'I'm sorry, very sorry. He hasn't been backed and turned away, Lynne. Some ignorant fool has taught him to rear.'

'How can you be so sure?'

'The look in his eye, the way he went up. It was calculated – not the action of a half-broken pony reacting to fear or a command he doesn't understand.'

I groped for words through the fog in my mind.

'When he came over backwards I thought he was going to fall on me. I saw myself squashed,' I admitted at last.

'He didn't mean to fall,' Briony told me. 'He toppled because you pulled on the reins. When ponies are vertical like that the rider must lean forwards and give them a loose rein. They're very finely balanced, you see – a jerk on the head or a shifting of the weight backwards is enough to bring them over.'

I asked whether he was curable and Briony said she doubted it, but we could try, and then I asked whether he was warranted quiet to ride and she said no, he wasn't, and she wasn't sure whether we could send him back. She would have to study the actual wording of his entry in the catalogue. She told me that she would now ride him herself, even though she was rather heavy for him.

'But supposing he topples with you?' I asked.

'I'm more experienced, and if he does I can probably throw myself clear. I shan't be taken by surprise. I shall be prepared. That makes a lot of difference. I wouldn't let you ride him again, and I certainly don't want David to have a go.'

My brain seemed to be misting over again, but I searched it for words and brought out a sentence rather slowly.

'You said "taught". Why should someone want to teach him to rear? He wasn't in a circus.'

Briony said she meant that some idiot had put Rocket into a situation from which he could only escape by rearing.

'It could have been a very severe bit,' she explained, 'or an ill-fitting saddle, or sore feet. You see if it hurts to be ridden, a pony must do something in self-defence. If a pony won't go you should look for reasons, not bring out the whip. I dare say they didn't shoe Rocket because they wanted to save money, and because all his hoofs became sore he didn't walk out lame, so they thought he was happy, whereas every step on hard or stony ground was actually hurting him.'

'But we weren't hurting him,' I argued.

'No, but he has become conditioned to think that being ridden is painful and so he's decided not to be ridden any more.'

'But he was all right when you were leading him.'

'Ah, but during the early part of his training his feet weren't sore, so he remembers that when someone was at his head he felt fine. It was only later, after he had been ridden out, that he began to suffer. But I'm only guessing, Lynne. I don't really know what happened. I wish people would gain a bit of experience before trying to break in ponies. You see . . .'

But now her face seemed to draw away again and her words grew fainter as the field tilted once more. I felt my knees giving way and the next minute the warm grass was all around me and then for a second there was darkness – a sudden nothingness.

'You'd better come indoors and lie down. Do you feel sick? Does your head hurt? Can you walk, Lynne? Lynne?' Her voice came to me from far away. I sat up; her arm was round me as she knelt at my side.

'My back hurts and my side – everything, everywhere,' I said, suddenly afraid that I might have to go to hospital and miss Candy's foaling. 'But it's nothing serious. I'm sure it's nothing serious.'

'Let's help you into the house. Up you get!' Briony heaved me to my feet, and once again the world straightened.

'It's my back. My back's hurting, hurting.' As I spoke I wished I wasn't repeating myself. 'I only

27

fainted,' I added.

'Better sit down. I'll fetch Mother.'

Rocket was wandering loose. Briony had put his reins behind his stirrups so that he shouldn't tread on them. I remember thinking that he looked intelligent and totally unconcerned with my difficulties. I scrambled to my feet as I saw Briony reach the garden gate. I don't usually make a fuss when I fall off but this time I felt peculiar and oddly annoyed. Suddenly the whole idea of the Pony Seekers seemed mistaken. Briony was always running into trouble. There was never enough money, and she was too trusting to make much from dealing with ponies. The more experienced people could run circles round her. I started to walk slowly to the house, putting one foot carefully in front of the other. Was this what being old was like, I wondered?

'Whatever's happened, Lynne? Darling, you look white as chalk. Come on, take my arm. Briony, go to the other side.'

Mother always kept calm in emergencies. As a one-time mountaineer, she was used to the possibility of accidents.

'She landed on her tail, the very last vertebrae. I should think she's horribly jarred,' Briony explained. 'She didn't hit her head and she can remember what happened, so she's not concussed.'

'No darkened room, then,' Mother said.

'I'm all right, just dazed,' I said.

And then Mother said that I was speaking slowly, which probably meant I was suffering from shock. A cup of sweet tea and a sleep would put me right.

Indoors she made me lie on a sofa so that she could feel me all over to make sure that no bones were broken. She made me move my arms and legs and bend all my joints. Then she looked at my gums and eyes to see that they were still red and healthy. She felt my pulse before declaring herself satisfied.

'Only your back is stiff. Briony's right. You've given your system a good thump from the base of your spine upwards and that's caused shock,' she announced. 'Let's put the kettle on.'

They gave me a mug of steaming tea and left me to sleep, and afterwards I woke up with a slight headache and a bruised back, but the dazed feeling had gone and my mind was clear. I announced ruefully that I had made too much fuss, but Mother said shock was strange and unpredictable.

'But I don't want you on that pony again. Rearers are not suitable for any children, however expert.'

I said I wasn't a child, but a teenager, which was different, and she said I was under eighteen and therefore in her care so I was not to argue. Then David appeared and remarked that Briony had been cheated again. She had left it too late to lodge a complaint about Rocket with the auctioneers as there was a time limit of forty-eight hours after the sale.

'She didn't read the small print in the catalogue. None of you did,' complained Mother. 'You children only learn by bitter experience. Sometimes it might be wise to come to us older people for advice.'

David then asked what exactly "turning away" meant, and Briony explained that it was not sensible to school a three-year-old pony strenuously or you risked splints and spavins, sprains and other forms of lameness caused occasionally by too much strain on young legs.

'So some people just back their youngsters at three and then turn them out for a year to mature, which means they are broken in, i.e. sittable on, but not schooled. The important point is that in the catalogue they used the term "backed" rather than "broken in". But I've told you this before.'

'So "turning away" actually means turning out for a

year,' David persisted. 'I do want to get everything absolutely straight.'

'Yes, of course,' said Briony impatiently.

'I think you would make an excellent lawyer, David,' Mother remarked, 'because you always want to understand the exact meaning of everything.'

'I must inherit it from you then,' David said. Mother had decided to study law and was to be articled to a solicitor in September.

'Maybe,' she agreed. 'But, sadly, you see, horse dealers seem to be as bad as second-hand-car dealers. There are always some cheats among the honest. It's obviously a very tricky business indeed. I think you're very brave to enter such a profession, Briony.'

'Or very foolhardy,' my sister commented with a wry laugh.

I said nothing, for the pain in my head had come back like a dull toothache above my forehead, and I was wondering whether Briony would ever raise enough money to rent stabling even if someone did answer her advertisement. The Pony Seekers, I reflected, galloped from one crisis to another.

4

The next Saturday's bright sunshine brought back Briony's natural optimism.

'I've got a feeling that we're going to find a winner today,' she announced, springing lightly into the truck's cab like a beautiful marmalade cat expecting to find a saucer of cream on the passenger scat.

'For heaven's sake, don't rush into things,' David advised. 'Look for trouble, fear the worst.'

'Oh, don't worry. I'm becoming very cautious. I shall be wary as a fox. I don't mean to be caught out again. For goodness' sake, I've suffered enough disappointment already!'

She started the engine, put the truck into first gear and turned gently into the road. 'Ten people wanting ponies. Isn't that great? Things are moving. And Mirabelle has a friend coming for lessons. Good old Mirabelle!'

'She's still bossy old Mirabelle too. She hasn't changed much, you know,' said David. 'She wants me to grow my hair and buy an electric guitar.'

'My dear, how very romantic!' I cried, my voice deliberately smooth and affected. 'Ask her to give you one for your birthday. She can afford it.'

'Looking for a new house,' muttered David.

'Who? What? Where?' Briony asked. 'I say, isn't this truck running smoothly?'

'Mirabelle – her father has decided that all the best people live in old houses with loads of atmosphere. He's

31

looking for somewhere quaint and comfortable, with space for a swimming pool.'

'You're joking!'

'No, definitely not, Briony. It's a hundred per cent true, but more or less secret, I gather. Their present house is already on the market, but not advertised. They're being terribly discreet.'

'I just hope Mirabelle will still be near enough for lessons. She's coming on so well, and her fees are quite a help. I mean they do seem to pay for all the fuel for this old truck,' Briony said, turning on to the main road.

Our first call was to see a lean chestnut who, Briony thought, might suit the secretary. Her owner was a nervous woman, owl-like in large spectacles with a nose like a bird's beak.

'I bought her for myself, but then found I hadn't enough time to look after her,' she explained.

'What's her name?' I asked.

'Plain Jane.'

'Because she has no markings, I suppose,' mused Briony, running her hands expertly down the mare's legs.

'Rather thin – worms?' David hissed in my ear.

'Her field looks rather bare,' I whispered back. 'Could be that.'

Briony's hands were now working their way round the mare's coronets with care, and the frown on her face suggested that she was perplexed.

'I'll fetch her tack,' offered the owner.

'No, please wait a minute,' Briony held up a restraining hand. 'I think there's a problem. Has she ever been lame?'

'Only once.'

'Do you know what the cause was?'

'No. She got better on her own.'

'Ringbone,' said Briony, straightening her back.

'I don't understand.'

'Plain Jane is suffering from ringbone. She's not sound. I'm sorry, but I can't buy her.'

The mare raised her golden head and looked sadly towards the road where a retriever dog was barking at a group of children playing on the grass verge. I wished we could take her home and give her to the secretary to ride and cherish at the weekends, because there was a sorrowful look about her which made me think her life had been hard. The woman asked whether ringbone was curable and Briony explained that many cases were these days. The success of treatment depended largely on where the ringbone was.

'Look,' she said, touching a hard knob which had formed on the pastern bone just above the coronet. 'I should seek a vet's advice. This has probably been caused by jar or arthritis, or the mare could have inherited a tendency to ringbone. It's not right on a joint so I should think she'll be all right, but I daren't risk that. She'll probably be lame again if she doesn't have treatment. I'm very sorry, because she's obviously a sweet mare and nicely made too. Thank you for showing her to us.'

We turned away as the woman took the headcollar rope, saddened because the pony's future now seemed uncertain.

'Do you think that woman knew?' asked David as we took to the road again.

Briony said she didn't know. Some people were awfully bad at noticing things. 'Get the map out now, will you, Lynne?' she asked. 'We're heading for Slipton-under-Catchwood to see a dun gelding called Nice Fellah, who might do for a family of four who want an experienced gymkhana pony.'

'Whereabouts?' I opened the map.

'Slipton-under-Catchwood?'

'Yes, but whereabouts is it?'

'Oh, about ten miles east of here, somewhere off the A
. . .' Briony quoted a road number.

'Here give it to me. Lynne's hopeless,' cried David
snatching.

'No, no, give it back. She asked *me*. You're a male
chauvinist pig.'

'Let Lynne have it,' said Briony. 'Don't quarrel.'

Slipton-under-Catchwood turned out to be a pleasant
grey stone village in the lee of a wood. The farm lay on
the outskirts, sheltered by tall lime trees. A girl of about
eleven greeted us, long and thin with a gap between her
two front teeth.

'You've come to see Nice Fellah, haven't you? He's
all tacked up,' she opened a loosebox door.

'Is he stabled, then?' asked Briony.

'Yes, just at the moment.' The girl led out a nicely
made dun with a dish face and black mane and tail.

'Why?'

'He gets fat and lazy on grass and, naturally, we're
afraid of laminitis.'

The answer was too pat to satisfy my sister, who,
catching my eye, raised her brows in a gesture of dis-
belief. The girl pulled down the stirrups.

'Who's going to try him?' she asked abruptly. Briony
said David, so my brother mounted and rode briskly
down to a large field where he walked, trotted and
cantered.

'He's very handy. Shall I test his wind with a gallop?'

'If you like. Yes, do, go ahead.' Briony's slight hesi-
tation seemed to suggest that she was suspicious. Had
she already seen an unsoundness? I liked Nice Fellah;
his sturdy good looks appealed to me. He was the sort of
pony who would keep going all day. The sort, I reflected,

which Fred admired – honest, tough and good-natured.

Away went David, faster and faster, the dun stretching his neck out willingly as he was gradually given his head, his long stride eating up the ground. David's hands slid up his mount's neck, he crouched forward like a monkey, his weight in the stirrups, his heels well down.

'He's a great pony – so willing,' the girl said.

'Why have you hogged his mane?' Briony asked. 'He's not a cob.'

'He has a little irritation there. The vet gave us some ointment.'

'Lice?' I asked.

'Oh no, nothing like that.' The girl spoke as though lice were a sign of neglect.

'They can catch them quite easily,' I said.

'Not here – we look after our ponies.'

'It's sweet itch, isn't it?' asked Briony severely.

The girl hung her head like a Saluki who has been discovered stealing food from a table.

'Just a little,' she admitted.

'And that's why you keep him in,' Briony continued. 'You know it's caused by an allergy, don't you? – possibly to certain grasses or midges – and that's why stabling and anti-histamine help. He's a lovely pony, but I must be totally honest with my clients. I'm an adviser rather than a dealer. They trust me. I can't let them down. I have no one on my books who would be willing to cope with sweet itch.'

David came back and Briony pointed out how the skin along the pony's crest, spine and dock had thickened into ridges and become scaly. 'Bringing him in off the grass has eased the irritation, but the evidence is still here. The disease was discovered too late and Nice Fellah will carry these symptoms for life.' Briony turned to the girl. 'I am so sorry,' she added. 'He's a beautiful pony, very clever. I'm sure you must be very fond of him.'

Patting Nice Fellah, the girl returned him to the stable without a word. The silence hung between us like a bad smell.

'Thank you so much for showing him to us. I'll phone you at once if any of my clients feel they can deal with sweet itch. I hope you don't feel we've wasted your time.'

'You said you wanted a gymkhana pony and you won't find a better one. His sweet itch doesn't stop him winning over and over again. You never get everything, do you? I mean, the more brilliant you are in one direction, the more likely you are to have drawbacks in another.'

'You might have to sell him for less,' Briony said.

'My Dad's not interested in haggling. He knows we've got a wonderful pony here. You can come inside and see all Nice Fellah's rosettes if you like. He's a pony in a million, he really is.'

'Yes, I'm sure he is, but sweet itch is an unsoundness and just now I can't buy unsound ponies. It's as simple as that. I'm sorry. Thank you very much for showing him to us.' Poor Briony always hated to say no, and now her words came out flat as paving stones and her eyes looked away at the truck.

'Thanks for the ride. It was great!' David added, as we climbed gloomily into the cab.

'A kind of eczema,' muttered Briony. 'The poor child was furious with us. I wonder how many other people have turned the pony down for the same reason? Was I horrible? I tried not to be, but I saw the sweet itch as soon as she brought him out of the stable. Oh dear, what a shame.'

David said she had been right but pointed out that Briony might find someone desperate for a pony to compete for the Prince Philip Cup, in which case might they not be willing to put up with sweet itch? Briony said possibly, but life would be simpler for her if she could find an animal without that rather disagreeable allergy. She must aim for perfection.

'Now, on we go. Someone get out the map, please. We still have two more ponies to see.'

'I'm thinking of Candy,' I said.

But Briony insisted that Melody would foal first. She was bagging up nicely and was due next week, possibly Monday. A vision of Candy lying sweating on the ground in agony flashed before my eyes – the result of dipping into too many veterinary books. If Candy's foal died during birth I should blame myself, because I had made myself responsible for her safety.

The next pony was milk white with a fiddle face, slightly lop ears and wise dark eyes with hollows above, which gave him a learned expression.

'He's not pretty, but handsome is as handsome does. He's a super ride, clever as a cat and quick on his feet. You can't fault him as a gymkhana pony,' his owner told us, standing at his head, a grey fringe of hair tumbling down her forehead. 'My daughter used to ride him, won scores of prizes, but now she's gone to college and lost interest – you know what girls are – and there seems no point in keeping him in the field doing nothing.

'He lives alone?' Briony asked.

'Yes, but he doesn't seem to mind. Now I thought you would like to saddle him up for yourselves to see how good he is. He never puts a foot wrong. To my mind he's a saint. He should be called Benedict or Francis, but actually he's called Silas.'

'I like that, it suits him,' said David, taking the bridle and martingale while I lifted the saddle off the loosebox door. Briony asked where Silas had won his many prizes and his owner said only at local shows because she didn't have a trailer.

'Emma used to take him to the ones within hacking distance. He's perfect on the road, by the way – doesn't even turn a hair at articulated lorries. His only drawback is his appearance. People want dishy little heads with bright eyes and perky ears.'

'Ah, but he's got character and he looks so wonderfully kind,' I said, meaning it.

'Oh, he is, the darling! He wouldn't hurt a fly, gentle as a kitten and wise as an owl – a real gem,' the woman said, her blue eyes very bright. 'He's sweet and I shall miss him. I always knew Emma was safe when she went out on him and such peace of mind means a lot to a mother.'

Briony rode Silas first, since he was fourteen hands two and up to her weight, and then suggested that I should have a try. He moved off with me briskly, his head a shade too high, as though his mouth had been roughly treated, his funny lop ears pricked as high as they would go. I soon found that he could canter very slowly at just the right speed for musical poles and that he was so sensitive to any movement of my body that I could swing him round simply by shifting my weight.

'He neck reins,' the woman said.

'Yes, he goes like a polo pony,' agreed Briony, who did not approve of the martingale attached to the bottom rein of a pelham bit. 'I think he would suit my clients very well. Could I possibly have him on a week's trial? I'll see that he's covered by my insurance policy.'

'But of course. We shall be delighted. We know you by name, and as far as I'm concerned, Silas is absolutely genuine and open to any trial. But he must have a good home. I shall want to know where he's going – that's more important than the money, although with inflation so awful, a bit of cash would certainly be useful.'

'Could you bear to part with him today? I'll give you a deposit,' Briony's green eyes searched the grey-haired woman's face earnestly. 'We like him very much. It's just a matter of showing him to a nice family who want a gymkhana pony. They have a stable, by the way, and a little old retired pony to keep him company.'

'Yes, but first you must come in and see his rosettes and his cups too— we're very proud of his cups.'

After a glass of sherry for Briony and squash for David and me and an examination of Silas's trophies, we drove out on to the open road again.

'What a co-operative and realistic person,' Briony sighed appreciatively. 'Misguided, because you shouldn't attach a running martingale to a pelham, but nice. And didn't Silas box beautifully! You can tell that he's been cherished, that he feels safe and sure of himself. Now we can take in one more pony on the way home. We'll be late for lunch, but never mind.'

But when we arrived at our final port of call, a man in well-worn riding kit told us that his pony had been sold earlier that morning.

'I tried to phone you but there was no answer. A bearded bloke with a lovely little girl bought him, paid cash and took him off in a trailer. No haggling, no argument, all settled in half an hour. Smashing!'

'Must have been a good pony, then. Never mind, we're not going back empty-handed.'

Briony sprang back into the cab, put on large dark glasses, for the sun was now at its peak, and started the engine.

'Well, David, I've kept within reasonable bounds, haven't I? Satisfied?'

'Let's hurry,' I urged, thinking of the mares again, as the truck started to climb a long hill, the road shimmering like wet coal caught in a torch's beam.

5

The family, who had imagined a dashing pony with the head of an Arab, objected to Silas's fiddle face and lop ears.

'He's like a floppy rabbit,' the eldest girl complained.

'Not really, Debbie, you clot. He's not cuddly but hard and muscled up,' her sister said.

'I want a black, a sort of highwayman's horse,' the third girl told us. 'You know, the sort of pony you see on book covers.'

'With white socks,' the eldest added.

'You can't expect beauty and talent unless you have loads of money,' Briony told them.

'All the same, maybe we should look a little further before actually buying,' the girls' mother said. 'We want a pony we can all love.' She opened the door of her white estate car. 'Hop in, girls!'

'He would have been perfect for them – so kind,' Briony lamented as they glided away. 'He would have welcomed them every morning with a whinny and slowed down if they lost a stirrup. Why are people so silly? Never mind, I'll ask to keep him a little longer. Lynne, there's a gymkhana a few miles away next Saturday. Will you ride him there for me?'

'Oh yes, please!' I said, feeling a little rush of happiness.

Today was Sunday. As I spoke church bells were ringing across the fields. Trees were nodding gently in a light breeze which sent small white clouds scudding across the sky like sailing dinghies. There was the smell of mown grass and tiny sun-soaked apples and flowers everywhere.

Candy was bagging up but not as fully as Melody, who Briony expected to foal in the next two or three days.

'I'll hang around,' she announced. 'She should breed a winner, but heaven knows what Candy will produce. I mean, who's the father? Did I tell you I rang Shaun Lester, the bloke who sold her to us, and he hadn't a clue? If the sire had been grand, the Irish would have sold her as a mare in foal instead of sending her over as a riding pony. Then there's the question of all those drugs she was given. Will there be side affects? I just hope she doesn't have a foal with no hoofs or two heads or something.'

'She'll be so sad if her child has to be put down. Animals don't understand when they lose their babies,' I said.

'Honestly, why do you both have to overdramatize everything?' asked David. 'Isn't there some old-fashioned saying: "Never worry worry until worry worries you"?'

While we talked Briony was saddling Rocket.

'He's a devil, a real devil,' she told us. 'But it's not his fault. Someone has mucked him up. He's determined not to co-operate. Probably, as I've said before, he associates being ridden with pain. Lynne, will you be an angel and lunge him with me on top? He was all right coming here because someone was leading him, wasn't he? Melody was in front too. So perhaps you would ride Silas out with me later on.'

The church bells stopped ringing as I led Briony on Rocket to the school, while Briony's lame show-jumper, The Mountain, watched us over the fence, his lovely coat dark and shiny as moleskin. But for him there

41

would have been a greater chance that we might keep Candy through the winter. Useless because of his recurring lameness, he would occupy one of the two looseboxes, consuming vast quantities of hay and earning no money in return. But he was a friend who had won fame and many prizes for Briony, and you couldn't dump someone just because he was lame. Loyalty, Briony thought, was a two-way commitment.

I had learned to lunge in the spring and soon I was standing in the centre of a circle with the lunge rein in my left hand and the whip in my right, making a small triangle with pony, rein and whip each a side and myself the apex.

'Walk on!'

Rocket walked.

'Trot on!'

He trotted, but with one eye rolling back as though he were monitoring Briony's performance, seeking any sign of weakness which he could exploit. After a time she suggested I send him round the other way. So I called him in, rewarded him with a pat and a pony cube and then turned him round, putting the rein in my right hand and the whip in my left.

'Walk on!'

Briony used her legs, but Rocket stopped with his ears back.

'Walk on!'

I made my voice louder and more dominating, touching him with the whip. And then he went up, straight as a circus horse, pawing the air. Briony leaned forwards, slackening the reins and repeating my order. Then she told me to use the whip again. I hesitated a moment as he came down, before obeying. A little snort escaped from his nostrils like the half-hearted backfiring of a car and the next moment he was upright again. This time Briony was ready and, bringing her hands down, she tried to force him back on to four legs.

'The whip!' she shouted, 'the whip!'

Needless to say, I hate hitting anybody, but this time I didn't hesitate, bringing it down across his thighs. There was an awful stinging sound and then he leapt forwards one stride before stopping dead in his tracks, his eyes rolling. I would have shot over his head like a stone from a catapult, but Briony stayed firm.

'Walk on!'

Our voices spoke together, but Rocket looked stubborn, planting his feet in the grass with a firmness which suggested glue.

'He knows what we mean. Touch him with the whip again, will you?'

I flicked him on the flank and, as if in retaliation, he went up again higher and higher, until I thought he must surely topple over, but he didn't, for Briony rode superbly. After what seemed like an age he came down again and she immediately used both legs and voice to try to persuade him to go forward.

'I'll lead him,' I said.

'All right.'

I stepped forward, put down the whip and coiled the rein and he nuzzled my pockets as though unaware that he had behaved disgracefully.

'He won't be any good for children,' remarked Briony gloomily. 'Once ponies know how to rear as an act of disobedience they're never safe. After a time I may train him to go for me, but there will always be at the back of his mind the knowledge that he can avoid doing what he doesn't like by rearing, and rearing, as you know, is dangerous. There's no way that I can recommend him.'

'So what will you do?'

'Send him back to the sale and let him take his chance.'

'He'll go for meat.'

'Possibly, but there isn't an alternative. I'm an honest broker, Lynne.'

'He's so pretty,' I said despondently. 'I mean, look at the shape of his head and his eyes – such intelligence.'

'Oh, he's clever, there's no doubt about that.'

'And his neat black hoofs set him off so well at the end of those sleek black points. Would you call him a raspberry roan?'

'Red, I think,' Briony said after a pause. 'It's the body colour under the grey hairs which counts. A strawberry roan is chestnut, but this little devil is nearer a red bay, isn't he? I don't think anyone uses the term raspberry. Now lead him on again, will you? We must finish on some sort of winning note. Then we'll risk trying him on the road with Silas. All right?'

'Yes, all right,' I agreed.

I led Rocket for a while and then I tacked up the grey and we went for a ride with myself in the lead. We took a shady road where the sun laced the dark tarmac with gold. Rocket followed Silas until he saw an old tin can in a ditch and then he stopped and reared again and I was terrified that he would fall over backwards and break Briony's spine. He didn't; he came down without mishap, but it took us twenty minutes to get him past the can, despite Silas's good example. The next time it was a broken dustbin which brought him to an abrupt halt and then Fred appeared as if from nowhere and made terrible noises, growling like a bear and shouting like someone at a rugby match. He waved his arms too, and eventually walloped Rocket with the staff he always carried, which seemed to be a cross between a walking stick and a shepherd's crook.

'Get on, you brute!'

Suddenly the air was full of oaths as Rocket repeatedly leapt forward three strides only to stop as soon as he was out of Fred's reach. In this way he proceeded past the dustbin, but reared again in terrified defiance as a lorry came round the corner. The next moment a car appeared, followed by a coach full of weekend trippers. All at once there was a traffic jam with Rocket in the middle, eyes rolling, fore legs pawing the air. Briony dismounted and led him to the side.

'Never do that. Never give in,' Fred said when the traffic had gone. 'This time you've been cheated, my girl! No mistake. Someone's made a monkey of you. But I'll tell you what we used to do with rearers when I was a boy,' his eyes glistened at the memory, 'we used to stick a red hot poker under their tails. That learned them! Or we broke a bottle of cold water over their heads.'

'Did it cure them?'

'A few, but not all. Some would only go on when they saw the poker, artful beggars!'

Fred gave Briony a leg-up. 'A nice-looking pony,' he added, 'but he ain't no good with that vice. He's only fit for pork pies.'

'Someone's mucked him up. It's not his fault,' Briony said, turning Rocket's head for home.

'I don't think those remedies will be much use to us, will they?' I asked.

'No, they won't make him reliable and I'm only interested in reliable ponies,' my sister said. 'See, he's all right now we're going back.'

I felt very sorry for Briony, having landed herself with a rearer, but my mind was really on Candy, whom I so desperately wanted to keep, so when we got home I decided that next day I would take Silas out in search of stabling.

'If we find a place by Christmas, will it be in time?' I asked. 'I mean, you won't wean the foals before December, will you? And you're not thinking of selling

45

either mare until then, are you?'

'Unless someone actually wants a mare with foal at foot, which seems madly unlikely,' Briony said. 'But now, Lynne, will you stop agonizing about the future? Everything's in the melting pot. Can't you understand? I live from day to day. I know you want me to keep Candy, but business is business. If someone comes along and offers me a fair price I shall sell her. So please shut up. I have enough problems here in front of my nose without looking ahead for trouble in December.'

'You'll be grey by the time you're twenty-five, Lynne,' warned David.

'You're both horrid, absolutely beastly!' I exploded, leading Silas away towards the field, knowing in my heart that Briony's anger was at least partly due to her disappointment with Rocket and that I was simply the ball that happened to be around at the right moment for a kick.

6

The next evening I ran to see Candy on my return from school, and she cantered across the field as usual with her long, easy stride.

'I'm going to search for stabling,' I told her. 'Briony hasn't had a single reply to her advertisement. Do you remember that time I rode you before you developed your second illness.' We saw empty buildings down a track – chimneys and a little square yard with ivy everywhere.'

She couldn't answer, of course, but it was nice to be able to speak my thoughts aloud without seeming to be mad.

'I'm going there on Silas, before I practise for the gymkhana,' I continued. 'Because if we don't find somewhere, Briony won't be able to keep you and your foal through the winter. Of course she's leaving everything to chance as usual. I don't understand my sister, Candy – she's marvellous, but she doesn't seem able to plan. It's very strange. And she thinks you're going to produce some puny thing which won't be worth a penny.'

While I talked Candy was searching my pockets in vain for titbits. I noticed that with the advance of summer, her coat was turning more golden, so that an elderly Irish woman who lived in the village was later to describe her as a yellow pony. 'You see them all over Ireland,' she was to add, 'tinkers' ponies hitched up behind caravans.'

'And who did you marry?' I asked Candy now. 'A beautiful Connemara with a flowing mane and tail? Or some ugly colt with cow hocks and monstrous head?'

But now Candy was moving away, having abandoned her search for pony cubes in the folds of my school clothes, and I walked back to the home fields to lecture Rocket on his foolishness before changing into jeans and boots and catching Silas.

The sun was drifting down the sky and shadows were lengthening as I turned the grey down a lane which wove its way through flat dry fields of corn within sight of the Malvern Hills. And it wasn't long before I reached the track I remembered and saw those tall chimneys sticking up above dark conifers. Here a notice read '*To Lambswood Manor Only. Private*', causing me to pause a moment. But, I told myself, I'm taking this way for a purpose. If caught I shall say I'm riding to ask the owners of the chimneys whether they have stables to let.

'Exploration, Silas,' I announced. 'Now we go into the unknown.' At first we continued to trot through flat corn fields above which the larks rose and fell like torn paper caught by a summer wind. Then we came to woods where a second notice warned that trespassers would be prosecuted. The scent of thyme and rosemary laced the air. Proud foxgloves, purple as bishops' vests, lined the path and bluebells ran like spilled ink through the undergrowth. I wondered why we had never considered before where the track led. A gate, heavily wired up with a board reading '*Private. Keep Out*', seemed to provide the answer. I dismounted and, determined not to forsake my self-imposed errand, scratched my hands undoing the wire. Silas stood patiently, head down, at my side like a horse waiting to be hired at a tourist resort. The stink of stagnant water from a still, green pond drowned all the wood's smells which had seemed so pleasant a moment earlier. Midges rose from the water like dust and buzzed faintly round my head. At last I succeeded in opening the gate.

'I'll shut it, but I won't do up the wire,' I told Silas. 'Come on through. Walk on. That's right. We're certainly not going to be made welcome in this place.'

Silas obeyed quietly, without fuss. His lips were grey, faintly blueish like the sharp side of flints, not pink-patched like Candy's, and his eyes had an old, knowing look about them, as though his experiences had been many and varied. Perhaps, I thought, he was no longer capable of surprise.

I remounted and pushed Silas into a trot. Minutes later we reached the yard and then the house, which seemed to rise out of a wilderness – a crumbling mass fighting a lost battle against the forces of nature. Its mullioned windows were boarded up. House martins and swallows chattered in well-designed nests under eaves and gutters, their droppings splashing the walls with white. Everywhere weeds triumphed in wonderful and wild profusion. The yard was empty of people but alive with insects and birds. Two magpies strutted like victorious soldiers at its entrance under a stone arch-way which had once boasted a clock. Nettles and willowherb grew tall as raspberry canes; ivy scrambled over the walls, sending its tentacles into every nook and cranny and turning mortar to powder. A shapeless elder tree shaded a high Victorian window in a stone shed which I suspected had once been the tack room.

I dismounted and, shooing the magpies, led Silas into the yard. Peering through a broken pane into the stable block I saw a row of stalls with blue Staffordshire brick floors and rusty mangers. A rotten ladder led precariously to a loft graced by a decaying dovecot.

But it was the tack room which aroused my curiosity with its squat chimney. The high Victorian window suggested wrought iron saddle brackets, a stone sink, a fireplace. I saw myself there in winter, warmed by a bright fire in a black-leaded grate, pinning rosettes on panelled walls. I tried the door, which creaked but held fast, fixed by a chain nailed either end. Not to be cheated of satisfying my curiosity, I tied Silas by the reins to a ring on the wall close to a decaying mounting block. I found a piece of old iron with which to lever up the nails and release the chain. Then with a sense of triumph I turned the handle, pushed back the door and stepped inside. For a moment I could see everything: an old wooden saddle horse, simple worm-eaten brackets, a neat rusty fireplace with chipped tiles, a tarnished lopsided tap above a cracked zinc sink. And then suddenly, as though a shutter had fallen, the bright light of day turned to semi-darkness as a gust of wind slammed the door shut. I turned and met the brown-eyed stare of a large rat, curious rather than fearful.

'Oh!' I don't mind rats. My cry was a moan of despair at the thought of imprisonment, rather than alarm. The rat ambled off to disappear behind the fireplace while I tried the door, but as I turned the handle it broke into several pieces, leaving only the end of a spindle which seemed to have slipped back into its hole. Sticking a finger in I tried to pull it out but the gap was too small for both fingers and spindle, and with a sickening little thud the spindle shot out and landed on the weed-covered cobbles outside. Now I was trapped. 'Help!' I cried in sudden panic. 'Help! I'm shut in. Let me out!'

Growing accustomed to the half-darkness, I saw a large leggy spider extending a web that hung like dirty gossamer at the high-barred window. Mice scuttled behind the walls happily going about their business. Insects were everywhere. This was their home. I was the invader, the alien. And now I was trapped. And nobody knew where I was. If night fell and my absence was noticed no search party would come here until all our usual rides had been visited. The place would take on a nocturnal life of its own; owls would hoot eerily in high branches, foxes would brush through the undergrowth and my tummy would rumble with hunger, while poor Silas would break his reins and explore the wilderness or wait patiently resting each hind leg in turn. And I would not sit down even though my legs might ache like rotten teeth, because of the insects and the rat droppings on the floor.

'I'm not afraid,' I said aloud. 'Only upset at the anxiety I shall cause.' But my voice sounded a little shrill and, even as I spoke, I felt the walls closing in around me until the tack room became just a box airless and musty – it is the musty smell which I still remember most keenly. Indeed I have only to catch the scent of bad yellowing hay to feel again the frustration which began to boil up inside me. I jumped and tried in vain to grab the bars at the window so that I could pull myself up to catch a glimpse of the yard, and at least see whether Silas was still waiting by the mounting block. But I have never had much spring and I soon went back to the door, disappointed but not surprised by my failure.

'Dear God,' I pleaded. 'Please show me where I can get out.' But in the same instant I rejected the possibility of an undeserved miracle, for I rarely went to church and said my prayers only occasionally when I felt in need of help.

Searching my mind for a cheery tune to hum to raise my spirits, I found a short stick to use in place of the spindle, but when I tried to turn it in the lock it broke in half, leaving the door firmly closed. Then I went round the walls feeling like a blind man in case there were loose stones which I could remove to make a hole large enough for my escape. But to my horror I only succeeded in disturbing a wasps' nest and then for the first time I felt terror rising like a scream in my throat. Covering my face with my hands I ran to the furthest corner from the nest; my heart pounding, my stomach tightening with fear. To be alone, shut in, was bad enough, but to share this solitude with a nest of wasps seemed more than I could bear. Their buzzing appalled me. I imagined that they were tangled in my hair, crawling down my neck, slipping into my boots. I struck out and was stung on the arm. One sting, I told myself, did not matter, but if they all set about me I should die.

I crouched on the floor with my arms round my knees and my head on my lap, trying to keep absolutely still so that the wasps would think I was a rock.

How long would it be before anyone worried because I had not returned? And what about Silas? Supposing he broke his reins? Would he find his way home or wander on the road risking a fatal accident? For, I decided, there must be a road to the house. Cars must have drawn up outside the handsome front door now flanked by crumbling pillars – carriages too, I told myself, deliberately trying to take my mind off the wasps who were indeed returning to their nest, having decided no doubt that I carried no nectar and meant no harm.

When all but a faint buzzing had subsided I opened my eyes again and straightened my back. Then I stood up, went to the door and started to kick it, calling 'Help! Let me out!' An answer came – a pathetic little neigh of the kind ponies use when they want to draw attention to themselves. 'I'm still here. Have you forgotton me? I'm getting bored and lonely,' Silas seemed to say, and I shouted back, 'It's all right, don't worry!'

'There must be a way to get out,' I told myself, hopelessly trying to squeeze my fingers between the door and its frame until the scratches on my hands started to bleed. Then, to my dismay, the sight of the blood seemed to release a well of self-pity inside me. I am ashamed to say I sat down again and, burying my head in my hands, gave way to tears. It all seemed so unfair when I had come only to help Briony, when I had wanted so much to be at home in case Candy foaled. If there was any justice in the world, I should have been rewarded for my efforts, not trapped in a dark shed full of rats, wasps and mice. And would I ever live down my stupidity in allowing the door to shut behind me? The very fact, I decided miserably, that I had landed in such a stupid situation proved that I was a fool. Or did it? Surely I could rise above my difficulties.

'I'm not going to be beaten,' I suddenly told the dusty air. 'Lynne Fletcher is not a coward, but a girl of action. Lynne Fletcher will be found fit and well.'

I sprang to my feet with new energy, peered through the hole which had held the spindle and called, 'Help! I'm shut in. Help! This is Lynne Fletcher, Lynne Fletcher locked in.'

The light was fading and now I imagined policemen tramping the woods in search of me, my parents anxiously touring the countryside by car, David on foot and Briony bringing The Mountain out of retirement to ride across the fields. And then miraculously I heard a voice – a man's voice talking to Silas, asking the pony how he came to be tied to a wall. Jumping up and down, I shouted, 'I'm in the tack room! Here! The handle broke and I got shut in.' And then there were footsteps, booted footsteps coming closer and closer, and I again imagined a policeman sent to search for me and I wondered if he would think me very stupid. What would I say? How could I explain? I was in the wrong, a trespasser who had ignored all warning notices, an idiot prying into other people's business. Now there were hands at the door pushing back the spindle, fiddling with the knob.

'It's only me, Lynne Fletcher,' I said, and then suddenly a thought struck me, sharp as a dentist's probe when it has found a painful hole. Could this man be a maniac, a murderer? Why am I so certain that he has come to rescue me? I moved away, crouched back against the wall, clenched my fists. And as though my fear had been conveyed to the nest a single wasp came out, buzzing importantly. The spindle turned; the door moved, a shaft of evening light pierced the gloom and there stood Fred with a gun in his hand, his thick brows raised in astonishment.

'This is private property. You've no right to be here. If you got shut in, you've only got yourself to blame, young nosy parker!' His blue eyes glittered as he hesitated, framed in the doorway solid as a bull, while, utterly astounded by his lack of sympathy, I searched for an answer.

'And what about you then?' I asked at last. 'Why are you here?'

'That's none of your business. Any cheek and I'll leave you in here overnight. Now then!'

'Now then, what?' I asked, trying to push past him.

'You've no cause to come here,' he said, barring my way.

'They'll be mounting a search party for me. They'll be here soon. And Silas is hungry, poor Silas. And look out because there's a wasps' nest in here. Look! I've been here hours and I'm terribly hungry.'

' "Trespassers will be prosecuted". Didn't you read the notice? Are you blind? I know you came the back way. I saw your hoofprints.'

'Are you in charge, then?'

'No, I'm not,' at last he seemed taken aback, 'and if you tell anyone you've seen me here, I'll . . . I'll . . .' He paused again, unable it seemed to think of a threat bad enough to frighten me.

'Oh, but I won't,' I said at once. 'And you musn't tell anyone you've seen me either. That's simple.'

'Not your sister, nor your brother, nor your father and mother,' he insisted, putting up an arm to prevent me sliding past him.

'No, I promise. I mean I'll try not to. Look out! You've woken up the wasps.'

'They don't sting me. They know better,' boasted Fred. 'What will you tell them then?'

'That someone I didn't know opened the door and let me out. A poacher perhaps.'

'You say poacher and I'll blow your head off.' Fred raised his gun, sending a sudden shiver down my back. Supposing he were mad?

'All right, just someone. Can I go now, please? I'm so terribly tired and Mother may have told the police to look for me and then they'll find you too.'

He stood back without another word and I ran to Silas, untied the reins and sprang into the saddle.

'It's quicker round the front,' Fred said, 'And there are no gates to unwire. The drive leads out on to the Frampton Road. Now remember, no names.'

'Don't worry,' I assured him, turning the grey, 'and thank you for finding me. Thank you very much.'

My heart was still pounding, I skirted the house, found the drive and sent patient Silas trotting for home.

7

What were my family doing? Why weren't they searching for me? How would they react to my story? I didn't know and now I was forced to lie about my rescuer. Fred, I decided, had been poaching and in the country that is quite an ordinary crime. It was odd that he had been so upset, which suggested something worse, but then he was a strange man who got things out of proportion. He had no judgement – everyone knew that. Otherwise he wouldn't go round the village blowing a hunting horn at four o'clock in the morning. But wasn't I an idiot too, for why hadn't I asked him who owned the stables? Now, after all my misery and uncertainty, I was coming back empty-handed. I had discovered nothing except that Lambswood Manor and its stable yard were empty and decaying and of some interest to Fred.

I was soon on the road with Silas trotting gaily with his head high and his lop ears pricked. My hands had stopped bleeding and I licked my scratches and wondered why nobody was looking for me. The sun had gone; birds had stopped singing. Petals had closed, but it was not yet dark. We were in that magical hour between sunset and night, when one half of the animal world is going to bed and the other getting up. Now, as our house came into sight, I strained my eyes to see whether the car was out or, worse still, whether any police were around. How awful it would be if a real search party had been mounted for me. If only someone had given me the dog for which I longed, I might have been able to send him home to summon help, if he had not been shut in with me.

Soon I came to the rented field in which we were keeping the two mares, and my first thought was to check that they were all right. Standing in my stirrups I looked over the straggly thorn hedge and was astonished to see both my parents, Briony, David and Mirabelle standing in a group, not looking for me at all.

'Hi!' I shouted. 'Sorry to be out so long. What's happened?'

They looked so solemn standing there that I was suddenly afraid that Candy had foaled disastrously without me.

'Where on earth have you been? Silas doesn't need so much exercise,' shouted Briony. 'I want you to practise for the gymkhana, not ride about the countryside all evening.'

'Your food's in the oven,' Mother said.

I reached the gate, rode through and galloped across the field.

'What's happened? Candy?'

'She's foaled.'

'Who?'

'Melody, of course.'

And then I saw that the small bay was in the centre of that dismal circle, contentedly nuzzling a mousey-coloured foal on the ground.

'Oh, and I missed it all! She looks fine. It's a day earlier than you expected, isn't it?'

'Sometimes the labour can come on very suddenly. Mares are terribly unpredictable. Each one is different, a law unto herself,' Briony said.

I dismounted. 'Let me see,' I pleaded, edging my way through. 'It looks all right. Why are you all so gloomy?'

'Just look carefully, then you'll see,' Briony replied in

her maddening elder-sister voice.

David took Silas. I knelt at the foal's head, while Melody eyed me.

'It looks all right. Why are you all so depressed? What's the matter?'

David looked at Mother. Father kicked a bit of turf with his left foot. A shortish, sturdy man, he could have been mistaken for a farmer, but he was an engineer and business man.

'Just look, look carefully and then you'll see,' Briony repeated curtly, her eyes averted.

Was he crippled? A spastic mongol foal? Half a dozen awful possibilities flitted through my mind like hornets with stings in their tails.

'Is he handicapped or something? His back is rather ridged. He's going to be dun, isn't he? There's a dorsal stripe and I like the dark yoke over his shoulders.' I was searching for a deformity. 'Is he a filly or a colt?'

'Neither, for all intents and purposes,' Briony said. 'Just stop being dumb and look at his ears. He's going to be dull brown.'

'Can't you see?' exclaimed David in disgust. 'I saw as soon as he arrived.'

'Well, not quite,' Mirabelle said. 'I think it took us all a few minutes.'

'We all know I'm the slow-witted one in our family,' I announced bitterly, my tiredness suddenly like a cloak of lead on my shoulders. 'He does have rather long ears and his face . . .'

'He's a mule, you clot,' David said.

'Our dear Briony's been done again,' Father observed sadly. 'His father can't have been a pedigree Dartmoor pony.'

'Now don't be too hard on her,' Mother said. 'We all make mistakes. We learn through our errors.'

'I've got the certificate from the stud farm. I checked

that before I paid for Melody. I'm not a complete fool,' Briony said.

'But the fact that she was served by the Dartmoor stallion doesn't actually mean she became in foal to him. She must have got out afterwards and mated with a donkey.'

'But the catalogue, Dad, the Fair Trading Act, or whatever it's called . . . surely . . .' my voice trailed away.

Our mother put on her new legal voice and cleared her throat. 'The entry in the catalogue,' she began, 'stated that she was *believed* in foal to a registered Dartmoor. The operative word, Lynne, is *believed*. Briony has no comeback. The owners may not have realized that she had fallen in love with a donkey. They may well have sold her in good faith.'

'Chance is against me. Chance is always against me. My life is never going to go right again,' complained Briony rather pitifully.

'Perhaps Candy will have a really wonderful foal to make up for this disappointment,' I suggested.

'But she hasn't got any papers. She isn't pedigree. She could have a donkey husband too. Anything can happen in Ireland.'

'Oh, that would be too much of a coincidence,' Dad said. 'Anyway, surely a mule isn't valueless? Perhaps the army would buy him.'

'Dad, you're being over-optimistic,' David observed drily. 'The army is more interested in guided missiles and the latest tanks. You know that. They haven't used mules for years.'

'But if petrol runs out. If oil refineries are destroyed. The possibilities, dear boy, are endless.'

'They breed their own mules, Dad – keep just a few at Melton Mowbray or somewhere. I remember someone telling me,' Briony said. 'Come on, I must make Melody a bran mash. What a strange bony little creature she has brought into this world. Next time you intend going on a marathon ride leave a note, would you, Lynne? We were planning a search party when we realized that Melody was just about to foal, and then I'm afraid you got pushed into the background.'

'Sorry. I went exploring. I got lost . . .' I began, but nobody was interested.

'We must think of a name for him,' David said. 'Perhaps we should call him after a pop group.'

'Why? Why on earth?' asked Mirabelle.

'Well, his mother's Melody.'

'He's bound to be ugly,' Briony observed. 'Mules are always ugly and they can't breed. They're hybrids. If you can think of a really ugly unmarried pop star. . . .'

'You're being cruel. He can't help being a mule. I think he's sweet and he's going to have a mealy nose, and look, he's got black donkey markings round his eyes.' As I spoke I felt near tears, not just for the new foal, but because I was hungry and tired, so that the disappointment of missing his birth seemed to be of mammoth proportions. And it was all my own fault. I couldn't blame anyone else. I hated myself.

'Supper's in the oven, rather dried up by now, I'm afraid,' Mother reminded me. 'You looked famished.'

'And pale,' added David. 'Perhaps you ought to start wearing make-up. Lots of girls of your age do.'

'I'm not lots of girls,' I replied with spirit. 'I'm me. I'm unique.'

'You can say that again,' laughed Mirabelle.

'Pale, but tough as old boots – it's often the way,' Mother said, putting an arm round my shoulders.

'Has the afterbirth come? Is it all over?' I took Silas's reins from David.

'Yes, and buried. She didn't need any help. She managed beautifully, just as I said she would,' Briony told me. 'At least we haven't got to pay a vet. Now, go on, give Silas a drink and small feed and then turn him out and have supper.'

But I didn't go at once. Instead I checked Candy, who was standing in a corner of the field looking very left out, having been shooed away by David. There were two beads like pearls on her teats.

'I think she's waxed,' I shouted.

'You're imagining things,' Briony called. 'I looked half an hour ago. She hadn't bagged up any more.'

'All these dreadful anatomical details!' complained Dad.

'Well, it's getting dark,' I admitted. 'And it doesn't seem very much. I mean, just spots really.'

Now I looked for hollows either side of Candy's tail, or any sign of softening in her pelvic region. Every so often she stamped a hind foot and swished her tail. Was that a symptom? My mind went back to the relevant page in the veterinary book I had studied, and I could not remember any reference to such behaviour.

'Lynne,' called Mother, 'if you don't go in and eat your supper at once I'm going to explode.'

'I'll look after Silas,' David offered. 'You look worn out.'

'She seems colicky,' I said.

'You're getting neurotic about that mare. Calm down,' Dad said.

'I'll check her before I go to bed, at midnight. All right? See, she's beginning to graze again,' Briony pointed out.

'A good meal and bed,' Mother added. 'We're all tired.'

8

I woke up. It was dark. A little rain spattered the window pane. My first thought was for Candy. I turned over and tried to be calm. 'Briony checked her at midnight,' I told myself. 'But we should have brought her to the home field. The vet said . . .' The house was very quiet. The silence was beautiful in the soft summer night. The rain had stopped now and I could smell the lavender bush which grew at the bottom of my window. For the hundredth time I wished I had a dog lying at the end of my bed or in a basket nearby. I needed a being with whom I could discuss my fears. In this way I might have cleared my mind.

'Half an hour's delay can be as dangerous for a foaling mare as two hours for a cow.'

Where had I read that? I turned over again and then switched on the light, which immediately attracted a sand-coloured moth. I dragged my watch from under my pillow. 'Ten past one.' If she foaled disastrously tonight and died I should never forgive myself. It could be that some strange telepathy between Candy and myself had wakened me, a message moving like a spirit across the great darkness of the night. My imagination soared; fearful pictures ran before my mind like a horrific ciné film.

My mother had once told me that it was the things you hadn't done which you regretted in later life – the omissions rather than the actions. 'Too late', she had declared, were the saddest words in the English language. Now the silence was broken by the lonely cry of an owl down in the copse by Mirabelle's house. A lorry's engine throbbed on the road. I got up, pulled jeans over my pyjamas, put on a sweater and crept downstairs. I picked up the heavy rubber-clad torch which hangs by the fire precaution blanket, pushed my bare feet into boots and slipped out into the cool darkness.

Walking down the lane, I was conscious of charcoal clouds moving across an immeasurable sky, and trees standing still like stones. The world was suddenly a stage waiting for lights, actors and audience to bring it to life. My torch's thin pencil of light caught a rabbit's white scut and I knew that all around me the nocturnal animals were living out their lives.

'Candy?'

My voice was like the trickle of a stream as I climbed the gate. Briony could be wrong about Candy as well as Melody, I thought. She wasn't a vet. She was a marvellous rider, but not an expert in all the different fields of horse management. Now I felt small and terribly unimportant, like a dot on the surface of the globe. But the next moment my flight of fancy was interrupted. Hoofs brushed violently through the grass as a horse, a phantom horse light as foam, came through the darkness at the gallop.

'Are you all right?'

I was astonished at my matter-of-fact tone of voice as I trapped Candy in the torch's beam and saw her flared nostrils, her wild eyes and sweat-soaked neck.

'Candy!'

I held out my arms as though I could catch her in them like a frightened child, but she flung herself at my feet with a groan, her sides heaving, her stomach enormous, her hoofs churning the grass into mud as her panting turned into squeaks which seemed extraordinary coming from so large an animal. I had a picture in my mind from a veterinary book of how a foal should arrive; forelegs first with the head resting on them, and now, looking at Candy, I knew something was wrong. For in the torchlight I saw that one hoof was pushing in the wrong place, causing a red ball-like bulge under her tail. My instinct was to stay to comfort and help her, but common sense bade me run. I vaulted the gate, pelted down the road, my heart thudding, and reached the house.

'Wake up, everyone! Candy is foaling and everything's going wrong – everything.' There was a trace of panic in my voice, because as usual I feared the worst. Briony keeps the vet's number on a card for emergencies, so I soon got through to the surgery, where a recording instructed me where to phone to reach the vet on duty. Next I had to look up a code, and by the time I had done that David and Briony were downstairs putting on shoes.

Sleepily, Thelma Wright, our nicest vet, said she would come at once. I grabbed a headcollar and tore back to the field with Briony following with sterilized string and scissors in case the navel cord needed tying and cutting.

'I had set the clock to look again at four,' she said, 'because her milk was running a little at midnight.'

Candy was lying on the ground with her teeth bared.

'She could die,' I said dramatically.

'Calm down!' cried my sister. 'You won't make a vet if you overreact. David, please will you run back and bring a bucket of warm water with antiseptic and the vaseline if you can find it?'

Then our parents arrived.

'She looks in a bad way,' Mother said.

'She could die,' I repeated. 'Foaling mares die more easily than calving cows. I've read it up.'

'We're more likely to lose the foal than the mare,' my sister told me. 'I wish David would hurry.'

'And Thelma Wright. What on earth is Thelma Wright doing?' I asked, kneeling down by Candy's head.

'She's got to dress and drive ten miles or so,' Briony said.

'Better fetch Fred,' Dad suggested, as those terrible squeaks of pain started again.

'She's pushing for all she's worth, but the foal's stuck. There's no time to waste and he's the only person nearby who might know what to do,' Mother agreed.

'But he hates us,' I cried, seeing again those angry glittering eyes at the door of the stone tack room, the gun glinting under his arm. 'He thinks I'm a nosey parker.'

'Oh, forget that! Don't hang around or you're going to have a dead foal on your hands,' Dad said. 'Even I can see that, and the mare's in pain.'

'Fred may hate you, but he loves animals, there's no doubt about that,' Mother added.

'Go on, Lynne,' urged Briony.

'No, I'm staying with Candy. I'm scared of Fred. Please go, Briony. Please be quick. I'm sure the foal needs turning round or something.'

Briony ran. Candy scrambled to her feet, circled twice and collapsed on the ground again.

'Labour pains. You've got to expect labour pains,' Mother said.

'One hoof must be in the wrong place. They should come out side by side,' I explained. 'Whoa, Candy! Gently, Candy! Help is coming.'

Then David came back across the field with a bucket and hurricane lamp. 'We need more light on the scene. How is she?'

'Terrible. Do you think I could turn the hoof round?'

'No, you could do more damage. Better wait for Briony,' Dad said firmly.

'But Briony was wrong,' I insisted. 'Briony doesn't know everything. It's all happening too high up.'

'She knows more than you,' Mother said. 'She's older.'

'Lynne, you're overdramatizing again,' David muttered gently.

'I don't know,' Mother said. 'She does look rather miserable and we're standing round like a load of half-wits. If policemen can deliver babies, why can't we deliver the foal?'

'Give me the bucket, please,' I cried.

I plunged my hands into the water, put vaseline on my arms and tried to do what I had seen a vet do on television, but I couldn't get a hand inside.

'Policemen are trained to deliver babies,' Dad said.

Then Briony came back.

'Fred's getting dressed. What are you doing, Lynne? Move over, let me have a go.'

She took off her coat, rolled up her sleeves, applied vaseline and soap, and disinfected her hands, but she was no more successful than I had been. 'I can't. There seems no room. She closes up on me,' she complained.

'Yes, same here.'

'Come on now, make way. Where's the soap? We'll soon put things right.' Fred had arrived. He flung his coat down. 'Hoof pushing out rectum. Could be serious. Must hurry,' he added. 'I've turned plenty of foals round in my time. You don't need no vet. Whoa, little lady! Steady there!'

He brought out his hands and washed them in the water. 'She'll be all right now. I've straightened the hoof. It's beside its mate now. The birth will be normal.'

'Why couldn't I do it?' Briony asked.

'You have to time it right, push in a hand between the

heaves. I've turned sheep and cattle too. It's easy once you know,' Fred beamed.

'Here comes the vet,' shouted David. 'I'll open the gate.'

'Late as usual,' growled Fred.

'That's not fair,' Mother said.

'I went to your house. You should have told me where the mare was,' Thelma Wright complained.

'My fault. I'm terribly sorry,' I said, feeling chastened.

'Then I saw the lights. I really only lost five minutes.'

Now the vet's car lamps lit up the whole scene. Candy looked round, her cheeks pinched with pain, her nostrils still flared, milk running from her teats.

'Hoof pushing against rectum. I brought it down. Look, foal's coming now,' Fred said, as Thelma Wright sprang from her car.

She took one hoof and Fred the other and, pulling gently, they brought out the foal, long, wet and dark as the night.

'It's a fine one,' Fred said.

9

After Thelma Wright had injected mare and foal with an antibiotic and anti-tetanus serum, she left to see a sick cow and we stood in an admiring circle to watch Candy, who prodded her foal with a hoof.

'Don't, you'll hurt him,' I objected.

'That's normal, that is. Wants to see what he's made of,' Fred told us. 'Go on, old lady, get the little devil moving.' The next moment Candy was guiding the foal in a circle with her knees.

'How very intriguing. Melody didn't do that. Perhaps it's an Irish habit,' Mother said.

'He's got to stand before he can suck. Well, I'm going back to a warm bed,' Fred turned away.

We looked at each other then, searching for words. It's hard to express gratitude to someone for whom you feel no affection.

'We're enormously grateful. You saved the foal,' Briony began rather formally. 'The vet might have been too late. We can't thank you enough.'

'It's not the first and I dare say it won't be the last. You've got a nice colt there, well bred I would say, make well over fifteen hands if I'm not mistaken. See what fine limbs he has! He's a lot better than that mule Briony went and bought at the Fair. Whatever on earth made you do that?' Fred turned to my sister, his thick grey eyebrows raised, his smile marred by the trace of a sneer. At that moment it seemed so sad that he could not be nicer, that he always spoiled everything with some spiteful remark.

Briony explained sheepishly about the certificate of service.

'But that doesn't guarantee a foal, does it? That's what you've got to look for – a certificate of guarantee. They didn't keep her at the stud farm long enough. Probably wanted to save money and then they let her get out with some rotten old donkey. You should have asked me for advice before you went. I could have told you. But then you young people are all the same these days – don't want to listen to your elders and betters,' Fred threw up his strong arms in despair.

'Well, goodnight and thank you, thank you very much indeed. We're all grateful to you,' Mother said. 'We shan't forget it. I'm off to bed as well.'

'Me too,' Dad said. 'What a night!'

The adults walked away, apart from Briony whom we never think of as grown up, but merely as one of us with just a bit more authority.

'We've got to get him sucking. He must have the first milk, that's very important. Look, he's fumbling,' Briony said. 'See if you can guide his mouth to the udder, Lynne.'

David held the hurricane lamp so that a shaft of light fell between Candy's hind legs, but when I got the foal's mouth in the right place, he only fumbled clumsily, too weak to draw the milk and too stupid to bend his head in the right direction.

'It's because he's had a difficult birth,' my sister announced at last. 'Melody's foal started to suck straight away.'

'Mules are tougher anyway,' David said.

'Who in this village has a baby's bottle?' Briony asked after a pause.

'Mirabelle's parents' housekeeper has a little boy,' David replied promptly.

'Oh brother, you know everything!' exclaimed Briony, laughing. 'You always have an answer.'

'Don't say that sort of thing or my head will get too big for my crash cap and a larger one could be pretty expensive,' my brother said. 'I've seen the girl stuff a bottle in the child's mouth when he keeps crying. It's a sort of dummy for him. I'll go and wake Mirabelle if you like.'

'It's half past two – an awful time to drag someone out of bed, but we can't leave this little guy without milk,' Briony said.

'He's tired. Look, he's lying down. Why don't we leave him to rest and get back his strength,' I suggested.

'He'll get weaker and weaker if he doesn't take the milk soon,' Briony argued. 'There's not a lot of time to waste. David, do you think . . .'

'Yes, all right. I'll go, of course I will, but I just hope I don't wake up Mirabelle's parents. Her father rather frightens me. He's so successful and so rich . . . Oh, I don't know . . . he's friendly enough.'

'On second thoughts, I'll come too,' announced Briony. 'He might not appreciate a boy throwing gravel at his daughter's window in the middle of the night. We'll leave you in charge of Candy, Lynne. Here's the torch. We'll take the lamp.'

The faint squelch of their feet on grass died away. The charcoal clouds moved silently across the ink-black sky and suddenly, as the stillness embraced me like a warm and fragrant cloak, I felt sure that I possessed a soul.

I left Candy for a moment to visit Melody, who was lying down, with her small mouse-coloured foal looking as though he had been roughly carved from wood by an amateur with a bluntish knife.

'You're sweet,' I told him, 'and precious, and some-how we're going to find you a loving home.'

When I returned to Candy she was lying down too, looking like a pale Chinese porcelain horse, with her foal folded up at her side. I wanted to sit down then to share their peacefulness. It made me wonder whether I had been a pony in an earlier life.

Then David, Mirabelle and Briony came striding across the field, preceded by the warm gold of the lamp's flame burning steadily in its glass prison.

'All sterilized and clean!' Briony waved a baby's plastic bottle. 'Up you get, Candy! Come on!' She pushed the comfortable cream body with her foot.

'She hasn't got rid of the afterbirth yet,' I said.

'Give her time.'

'Oh, what a pity to move them when they look so comfortable,' cried Mirabelle. 'Why don't you leave them? What a dear little foal! I'm so glad you woke me. Is he grey? He looks grey.'

'Sort of sludge colour. Could mean anything,' David said.

'But with white socks and two-coloured hoofs, do you see?' I put in.

'What an exciting night you've had,' said Mirabelle, her uncombed hair wild and flyaway like a red halo round her head.

'He must suck or his inside won't function properly,' Briony said sternly. 'Sometimes one has to be cruel to be kind.'

'You sound like an old-fashioned nanny,' Mirabelle giggled.

'It's not a joke,' retorted Briony, rather irritably, as she started to milk the mare.

After much persuasion the foal took two pulls from the bottle and then gave up.

'Not enough,' my sister said. 'We must persevere.'

So we went on trying until a skein of pale grey un-wove its thin strands across the sky, spreading soft light across the darkness, and the trees became trees again, and Fred's bantam cock started to crow, boasting that he had six fine wives and a run twenty feet square. And then it was as though every bird in the world had started to sing, and a great blanket, pink as pearls, spread across the eastern sky.

'I'd quite forgotten how beautiful dawn can be!' Briony exclaimed.

'He's not going to suck – any fool can see that,' David said flatly.

'Well, now it's light I shall ring the vet again. There's no other way. I don't want this foal to die,' Briony said. 'Let's go and make a pot of tea. I'm famished.'

'I'll stay with her,' I offered. 'Someone must watch.'

'Will you trust me?' Mirabelle asked.

'I only want to know whether he sucks while we're away. It's just possible that he might suddenly summon the strength to do so and then we shan't need the vet,' Briony explained.

'Yes, I can do that. I have two very good eyes – six-six vision actually,' Mirabelle said. 'David, you creep, why don't you do up the bottom button of your shirt?'

10

Thelma Wright, stocky, blue-eyed and calm, fed the foal by tube. I poured Candy's milk from a plastic jug down a funnel attached to the tube, which had been inserted through the foal's left nostril and ran right down into his stomach. Briony held the foal and David held Candy, who was very agitated to see her baby treated in this way.

'There, now. He'll be all right now,' Thelma Wright said when the jug was empty.

'It wasn't a lot of milk,' David observed. 'Hardly a pint.'

'No,' the vet agreed. 'Mares don't carry as much at a time as cows do, so their children drink little and often, but it's very strong, nutritious milk. What a night you've had! How are things otherwise?'

Looking melancholy, Briony explained about the mule.

'See,' she said, pointing. 'He's quite an oddity.'

'But there must be a slot for him somewhere in life,' Thelma Wright insisted, walking over to examine Melody and her foal. 'He looks healthy enough. Anything else wrong?'

Briony gave her a lively description of Rocket's bad behaviour, for which the vet could offer no remedy. Rearers, she said, were the devil.

Candy's foal was now walking about the field, looking astonishingly confident, despite a slightly wobbly gait, and Thelma Wright decided to take away the afterbirth before she left – just to be on the safe side. The contractions which followed were horrible for Candy, who lay stretched out for a few moments with her lips drawn back and her teeth bared. Then, suddenly, the pain ended, she sprang to her feet and started to graze and I relaxed for the first time since one o'clock.

Briony reminded the vet that she was looking for stables to rent and then we went indoors and cooked ourselves a substantial breakfast of bacon and eggs while discussing again the possible names for our new arrivals. I said that the mule must have a pretty name, because if you were ugly it was all the more important to sound attractive. David accused me of talking rubbish. A pretty name for a mule would be most misleading.

'Post!' he cried, as letters fell on the mat.

'School!' called Dad from the passage upstairs.

'Oh, let them have the day off,' Mother urged. 'Say they've been studying nature all night – that will be the truth.'

'Here we are – two for Briony, three for Dad. None for Lynne and me – typical!' David put the letters down on the table.

'Do you really mean we don't have to go to school?' I asked.

'Yes, yes, we'll give you a letter to take tomorrow,' Mother replied, coming into the room. 'Any news? Anything nice?'

'Yes, yes, oh goodness, yes!' cried Briony, her green eyes bright. 'Someone wants a pony for breaking to harness – an animal with a wide chest, good action and a neat head.'

'Not Silas,' I said.

'No, Rocket. He'd make a terrific harness pony. I can just see him pulling a gig – right build, everything.'

'But won't he rear?'

'Not if he's well broken. He's conditioned to rear with

74

a rider,' Briony told me. 'He'll be in a different context between shafts and it won't occur to him.'

Crunching toast, David wanted to know whether she would tell the prospective buyer about Rocket's vice.

'Of course, otherwise he might land up breaking a child's neck, and then I shouldn't sleep at nights. He's a super pony to look at, and might well win prizes in harness. I shan't lose out.' Briony rubbed her hands together. 'Perhaps things are looking up at last; perhaps we shall even place that poor little mule. Now, Lynne, what about Silas? I want you to practise properly today, because I hope to sell him at the gymkhana on Saturday.'

I said I would ride the grey if someone would help me to put up bending poles and would hold potatoes for me, and that sort of thing. 'I need the record player for example, don't I?'

'It had better be me, I suppose,' David said, 'because Briony has that letter to answer.'

I almost danced down to the field to catch Silas, because I was so happy that Candy was safe with a beautiful foal, despite all her earlier troubles. The light now was clear and pure; white chiffon clouds rode high in an azure sky. Diamonds of dew caught and reflected the first rays of a rising sun. Everything smelt fresh and untarnished.

Scrambling from the gate on to Silas's back, I rode him to the yard and put him in one of our two loose-boxes. If only there were ten, I thought, what bliss then. As I saddled the grey, Mirabelle's red hair appeared over the door.

'I say, Fred's boasting like mad. He's told practically the whole village that he saved young Briony's foal. He stood in the middle of the road, trapping the people as they set off for work.'

'Well, why shouldn't he?' I said. 'He needs to be a

success; perhaps it will make him nicer. And how are you? How's the house-hunting?'

'Oh, that.' Mirabelle sent a stone spinning across the yard. 'I don't want to move. I like being near all of you. I like being taught by Briony. Dad's so changeable. I never know what he's going to do next. You see he has enough money to alter his lifestyle whenever he wants. I'm always afraid he may suddenly announce that we're all going to live in the Bahamas or something. Only my education is holding him back. I think he's on the scent of a place now, but he's got to consult architects. He's a business man, so he does actually look before he leaps. I'm insisting that I must be within riding distance of Briony.'

'Very flattering, thank you,' I said, leading Silas out. 'But you know as soon as Briony clears up one problem another arises. But I'm glad she decided to give the Pony Seekers another try – she nearly gave up after the strangles; I just wish she were more dependable. Now she's worrying about stables. She needs more loose-boxes or she threatens she'll close down for the winter.'

'And that means she'll sell Candy,' suggested Mirabelle with sudden understanding. 'And then you'll be sad, because you have a special feeling for that mare, haven't you?'

'Absolutely. I've nursed her through two illnesses and that makes a sort of unique bond.'

'Dad says Briony has got to learn self-discipline. He says she's too impetuous and emotional at the moment to make a good business woman. She does things on impulse.' Mirabelle's cool, blue eyes were candid as plate glass. 'To be landed with one mare in foal is bad enough, so why double it by buying another?'

'Two foals are happier than one.'

'Yes, but he says business isn't anything to do with happiness.'

'But life is,' I declared, mounting.

'The fact is,' Mirabelle went on relentlessly, 'Briony shouldn't have started a business without proper stabling. Look what a mess she was in this spring with no shelter for sick ponies. She's never prepared for the worst.'

'She's only first-year-student age,' I pointed out.

'Then your Dad should have controlled her, but of course, his firm's in a mess too, isn't it?'

'I don't know,' I replied uncomfortably. 'It was, that's why we started the Pony Seekers, to pay for our own animals, especially The Mountain.'

'That horse is not earning a penny. You should use him for advertising or something. Dad's a very astute business man. He never puts a foot wrong. Just now he's thinking of buying a golf course, and you can be sure that whatever house he eventually finds for us will double its value in no time at all. He started with nothing but a hired lorry. He left school at fifteen and built up everything in eighteen years.'

'A little help. I need help, would you mind, Mirabelle?' I asked, disturbed by the direction of the conversation. 'Could you possibly stick up the posts again if I knock them down when I practise bending, and stop and start the record player? You see, David has put everything out for me and then gone off with Briony to look at a pony for the secretary. And could you please hold those potatoes for me, so that I can gallop up, take them from you, pelt back and drop them in the bucket in turn?'

'No problem. I'm very grateful to you as it happens, because my night up has let me off school. When Mum heard you weren't going she said I could stay too.' Mirabelle's smile was so wide in her rosy face that I thought of tomatoes splitting in the sun.

I started practising and soon found that Silas was

much more expert than me. When I galloped round a bucket with a potato in my hand he leaned inwards as he turned so that I only had to drop it a few inches into the bucket, and when Mirabelle stopped the record player he would swing in towards the poles without being asked. Indeed, his reactions were so quick that each time he took me by surprise. As for bending, he would turn so close to the top post that I had to be careful not to knock it with my knee.

'He's unbelievable!' I gasped. 'He knows it all. He's even quicker than our little Nugget was . . . you remember? The pony David and I learned on.'

'Oh, he was sweet. If only this one were prettier,' sighed Mirabelle. 'I do so love pretty ponies.'

'But he's so obliging, so good and patient,' I cried, swinging from the saddle. 'I shall hate to see him go.'

11

Briony and David returned with a kindly dappled bay mare of thirteen with a slightly hollow back and black points. She belonged, they told me, to a riding school and now needed a new home with lighter work.

'There's nothing wrong with her,' Briony explained. 'She's just bored stiff because she's been teaching people for eight years and knows it all. Her owner, a nice imaginative girl, says a new home will rejuvenate this mare. At first she'll be very obedient and quiet and then, just when the secretary is beginning to decide that she's a riding school slug, she'll start to liven up, you'll see, and by then her new owner will be able to cope with a few high spirits. She's steady as a rock and absolutely genuine.'

'You're picking up dealers' jargon,' complained David, who is good at English language and literature. 'I never thought you would. You'll be saying "jumps like a stag", "goes like the wind" and "straight as a die" soon.'

'Oh, dry up, brother or I shan't take you to see the stables I've heard about.'

'Oh, where, Briony? What? How?' I cried. 'You never told us.'

'My advertisement – you remember my advertisement? Well, somebody has replied at last, just when I was giving up hope – ten looseboxes, forage room, tack room and garage – sounds like a dream come true, doesn't it? Come on, turn out Silas and pile into the truck!'

'Rent?' asked the practical David. 'I bet it's too much for us.'

On the way to the stables Briony asked me about Silas and was pleased by my reply.

'His owner says I can keep him a little longer. He won't be hard to sell. He's a pony in a million,' she said.

The wooden looseboxes were set in a square, well gravelled yard which we entered through double gates. An apron of concrete fronted all the buildings. Each loosebox had a barred window, kicking boards, a modern manger and an automatic drinking bowl, as well as a ring for tying the horse during grooming. The floors were grooved concrete, sloping very slightly to a drain which ran along the bottom. The tack room was also well equipped with plenty of hooks, steel saddle brackets and a new-looking saddle horse for tack cleaning. There was a sink in one corner and two electric points.

'All very modern and up to date, no water buckets to carry,' mused Briony. 'A super place, just what I want, but there's bound to be a snag. Dreams don't come true. I like the overhang above the looseboxes which means the horses can look out without getting their heads wet. And the yard's so sunny.'

I said nothing, because I was thinking of the drawbacks to Lambswood, whose charm, despite my imprisonment, was still with me.

'Absolutely purpose-built,' Briony continued. 'Wonderful! The very sight makes me feel businesslike. You can charge more when you have a setup like this. How can I function properly with only two looseboxes?'

'The foals could share the box next to the tack room. It's the largest,' I said.

'Yes, twelve feet by twelve; the others are only ten by

ten,' Briony said. 'But The Mountain really needs that one. This yard has been used as a livery stable, mostly for ponies. There are two paddocks included with it and the chance to rent an additional six acres.'

But, she added, there was bound to be a delay because the owners had gone bankrupt (was that a bad omen?) and there was a legal wrangle going on. She said they would probably sell the stables eventually.

'And then we'll have the same problem all over again,' David complained.

'I shall; you won't. Perhaps I can afford to build by then.'

'I can see myself working in this yard,' I mused, 'sweeping up, carrying haynets from that forage room, riding Candy and teaching the foals to lead in hand.'

Briony stared at me for a moment as though I were a stray dog who needed to be seized by the collar and led back home.

'The mule's going,' she said baldly. 'I don't want my failures staring me in the face.'

'Not now? Not at once?'

'No, but as soon as I can wean him, in four or five months. Unless someone wants the mare with a mule at foot, which is wildly unlikely.'

'But then Candy's foal won't have a companion. I thought you said . . .'

'Too bad. Things have changed, haven't they? A Dartmoor pony is one thing, a donkey's child is another. I want to start here with a clean sheet, Lynne. All right?'

'You're becoming like Mirabelle's dad,' I said. 'This place could do with a tree. It lacks atmosphere.'

David laughed. 'Briony's running a business, not a garden centre.'

'You're getting like Mirabelle's father too,' I said.

'That means we'll be making some money then,'

David rubbed his hands together. 'We need more men like him around to bring the country out of its slump.'

'And then more people will have more money to buy more ponies,' added Briony. 'Come on, let's go.'

After tea I walked down the lane to see the mares. Candy came at a trot, her foal following. Melody waited to be approached, her mule looking like a wooden toy to be pulled on wheels, with his slightly stunted walk and tough inelegant head. Each of his ears had a dark line running along its back and his eyes were encircled by the same shade as though someone had tried to enhance them with make-up. His nose was wheaten as though he had just plunged it into a bag of wholemeal flour.

'You may not be delicately made,' I told him, 'but you're a charmer. You're cuddly and sweet. Don't take any notice of what people say. If they criticize it's only through snobbishness. I'm going to be a vet, so I shall care for all animals, whatever their breeding. You've got to love all sorts to be any good in that job. An old mongrel needs as much care as a young champion from Crufts.'

I tried to touch him, but he moved away – born, it seemed, with a distrust for human beings, whereas Candy's foal was astonishingly friendly and not the least afraid of me, as though I had been his friend even before birth. Musing on this I went indoors to see what Briony was rustling up for lunch. The morning had been the longest of my life.

12

The day of the gymkhana seemed to arrive with amazing speed. I hacked over in sunshine, entered the field and found myself being called almost at once to line up for the Walk, Trot and Canter Race.

'On your marks. Get set. Go!'

Silas's stride was generous and sure, his neck stretched out, his lop ears raised as far as they would go. He felt long and low and I gave him all the rein he wanted. As we turned at the end, he broke into a trot without being told, but, despite his enthusiasm, he was soon overtaken by a dun who looked as though he could keep trotting all day. Moments later we were galloping on the last stretch, but the distance was too short to allow much speed and the dun passed the winning post first with the rest of us still in pursuit.

'Second. Well done, Lynne! Did you recognize the winner?' Briony was at the ring side, her loud voice an embarrassment to me. I dismounted and, patting Silas, rewarded him with three cubes.

'He does it all. He's a genius,' I declared. 'No, who was it?'

'Nice Fellah!'

'Oh, heavens! I wish I had won!' I declared.

'We've met Silas before,' one of my rivals said, cutting in, 'but with a different rider. He should go in for the Prince Philip Cup. But the girl who owned him couldn't be bothered.'

'Well, he's looking for a new home,' I said, 'but it

must be a good one.' I glanced at Nice Fellah's rider, who wore a pleased smile.

'It's a pity about his ears!' said a snooty-looking girl in a fashionably cut raincoat and high heels. 'I mean he's not very decorative, is he?'

'He's got character, that's more important,' I retorted, and then I had to mount for the Bending Race, and Briony tightened my girth. My first line of posts didn't look quite straight, but Silas had no difficulty in winning his first heat and then the two which followed. When I went to collect my red rosette, the judge, a middle-aged woman with a pug nose, said that I seemed to be carrying off all the prizes today, so I said, 'Not me – Silas,' which was perfectly true.

'You still have to stay on top,' she insisted.

The Potato Race was next and, lining up with five other riders, I felt confident and relaxed. Silas, I told myself, was the most obliging and cooperative pony I had ever ridden. At the drop of the flag, he leapt into a gallop and we were first to reach the people holding potatoes for us. We were in the lead the first time we turned round the bucket too, but the second time was a different matter. Silas leaned over, swinging round it like a polo pony, a little sweat lying on his neck like soapsuds, but he was too quick for me. I dropped the potato a second too late and it fell in the grass with a sickening soft thud. I brought Silas to a halt, leapt off, grabbed the potato, remounted and chucked it in, but now three of the five ponies in my heat were ahead and we only caught up with one of them. Nice Fellah won again and his rider grinned triumphantly, so now I was out of the finals.

'You didn't practise enough,' Briony said.

'Easy to be wise after the event. I'm sorry.'

'Nugget was so much smaller that our hands were nearer the bucket,' David reminded me of our first pony who had taught us so much.

'He was also not quite so fast. You should have ridden Silas, not me. You wouldn't have missed.'

'You should have bought this one after all,' Nice Fellah's owner said with a smirk. 'He's faster and handier and his ears don't droop.'

'He's super, I agree, except for the sweet itch,' Briony said.

I felt very angry with myself for letting everybody down.

'I expect I would have dropped a potato too. Anyway, it was your turn. I had all the responsibility with Starchaser,' David said, recalling a previous pony he had jumped for Briony.

'No one would come and hold potatoes for me. Mirabelle did once, but you were always doing homework or something. I *wanted* to practise more,' I searched for excuses

'You musn't blame other people,' Briony told me sternly. 'One must learn to be a good loser. Now keep your eyes and ears sharp for the Musical Poles. I want to sell this pony today. Remember to canter very slowly up the short stretches and quickly at the corners when you're furthest away from the poles, and look out for Nice Fellah!'

'I don't feel on top of the world,' I complained.

'Nobody does just before an event, dumbo!' retorted Briony. 'Good luck! Listen, they're calling your number.'

'My tummy is eating itself,' I grumbled.

'Nervous indigestion,' my sister said.

There were thirty-five ponies entered in the Musical Poles, so that there was rather a scrum in the beginning, but Silas was not afraid of pushing. Once he had selected a pole as his own he would approach it with his ears flat as plaice, swinging his quarters round with a swish of his tail to clear the area of rivals. 'This is mine,' he seemed to say. 'Stay at your peril!' His hearing was perfect; he would notice before I did when the music stopped, even at the furthest corners, and his acceleration was as quick as a sports car's. On one occasion we were nearly caught out at a corner; we thundered in only to find the other eight riders before us, but one young woman fumbled when she went to grab a post and it toppled to the ground. Leaping off, I was able to grab it firmly before she had decided what to do next.

Eventually there were only two of us left and then we were send round in opposite directions. My rival was a teenage girl on a clever dun gelding — Nice Fellah, of course! We were both on the long stretch on different sides of the ring when the music suddenly faded. Had it stopped or were we simply out of earshot during a quieter part of the record? I wasn't sure, but Silas knew. Swinging in, he raced for the single post, his eyes threatening, his tail swishing. As we arrived, the other rider's hand was outstretched, but Nice Fellah hesitated, frightened by the threat Silas seemed to pose, and the next instant I had the top of the pole within my grasp. People started to clap. We had won.

'Well done! You were brilliant,' David exclaimed with rare enthusiasm.

'Your pony threatened mine,' Nice Fellah's owner said, a scowl on her hot forehead.

'He never kicked. He wouldn't have kicked. He isn't a kicker. It's just the look on his face. I'm sorry, but there it is,' I said. 'The most courageous pony wins.'

'I think he's got a home,' Briony said, when I came back with another red rosette. 'A lovely family, two girls, very keen. They've just had to retire a beloved gymkhana pony through lameness and they both hope to compete for the Prince Philip Cup. They're twins. They're coming to try him tomorrow. And they actually like his ears!'

'And his fiddle face?'

'Yes, that too. They say he has a learned look. Their father is a professor, so they're used to scholars,' Briony laughed. 'Do you want a drink, Lynne, before you ride home?'

'Squash would be gorgeous,' I said. 'But Silas needs something too.' I dismounted and patted his hot grey neck. 'I wish we could keep him. I wish you had signed a lease for stables and that we could fill them with horses.'

'If you had your way we'd never make any money,' Briony laughed. 'Well done, and thank you. But do remember, no sales means no stables.'

'If only we were rich!' I sighed.

13

Riding back on Silas I thought of the neat stable yard, contrasting it with the more romantic but broken-down place I had found. Stone, I told myself obstinately, would be warmer than wood, and my overgrown yard was both nearer and more sheltered than the one Briony had found. But would a paddock go with it? And what had Fred been doing there? And was it to let? Wasn't I building castles in the air?

Trotting through shady woods, I decided to pluck up enough courage to tell Briony about my adventure at Lambswood Manor and then to find out who owned it. Fred would know all the details, but did I dare approach him? And, if we didn't find anywhere, who would Briony keep? The Mountain, of course, but otherwise one mare or both foals? No, the mule must go, poor little mule. She might decide to keep Candy or Melody, or a gelding, who would be more suitable company for The Mountain. Or nobody. It would be cheaper to keep nobody and then start with a clean slate in the spring. That would make business sense.

When I reached home I found my sister driving Rocket on long reins made from clotheslines.

'I'm preparing him for his next owner. You see, he's quite docile and he won't be frightened of things in hedges and ditches when he's wearing blinkers. He's got a great trot, and just look at that chest and shoulder.'

I asked her about the stable yard and she told me she was waiting for the estate agent to ring her back. He had another interested client. Then she had a phone call which David took.

'Quick! Might be exciting,' he said. 'You did very well,' he added to me.

'Thanks.'

I paused as I unbridled Silas. David was obviously in a good mood. Should I tell him? I glanced at his face and saw that he was still smiling. The rain had gone and the fields looked very green under the July sun.

'Listen, you know the night the mares foaled . . . you know I was terribly late back . . . I was looking for stables, you see. . . .' Bit by bit I told David what had happened, half-breaking my promise to Fred.

'We'll go this evening,' he said when I had finished. 'Yes, why not?'

'To look?'

'Yes, on bikes. You can borrow Mirabelle's. She won't mind.'

'We seem to be leaning rather heavily on her these days.'

'She likes it, Lynne. Everyone likes to feel needed, even me. We won't tell Briony, not yet.'

'Supposing we meet Fred?'

'I'm not afraid of Fred. Anyway, he'll be in a good temper because Briony's given him a hunting horn. You know he lost his last one?'

'The village won't thank you. Is it the one from upstairs?'

'That's right. The one a fan sent her, very new and shiny. We're trying to thank Fred, not the village. It's what he wanted most. No good giving him anything else.'

Then Briony came out of the house with a broad smile on her face.

'Good news!' she called.

Not a home for Candy, please, not a home for Candy!

I secretly pleaded with Providence or Fate or whatever it is that decides our future.

'The people wanting Silas, I expect,' suggested David, pushing back fair hair from his face. 'Phew! What weather!'

'Thelma Wright – she's found a home for our little mule.'

'I don't believe it!' cried David.

'And why not?' I demanded. 'Why shouldn't someone want a mule, an intelligent and strong animal?'

'A wonderful home,' Briony told us, beaming. 'The farm park. You know, the place with long-horned cattle, oxen, game cocks and ancient boars – wild boars like those Henry VIII used to hunt.'

'Great!' said David. 'Another load off your mind.'

'But Briony,' I reminded her, 'you bought Melody so that her foal could keep Candy's company. The fact that it's a mule doesn't mean to say it can't be an excellent playmate and companion.'

'Calm down, Lynne. You know I expected a pedigree pony, not a mule, but apart from that, the Warden says he'll have Candy's foal for the winter, so that the two can be together. So the mission is to be completed without costing us a penny.'

'Does that mean you can keep Candy for me, if I manage to raise the money to buy her?' I asked. 'You owe me half the selling price of Nugget, and if I get a really good summer job I should raise a lot more.' Nugget, who had belonged to David and me, had been sold, partly to get Briony out of a fix, and she still owed us the price he had fetched.

'I don't know. It depends on whether we get stabling and how much I make buying and selling. I'm still living rather hand to mouth. I'm sorry not to be more definite, Lynne, but I can't keep a pony for you and not one for David. Hay's going to be very expensive this year, despite the good weather now – the spring was so late.' Briony patted me on the back. 'I'll do my best and thank you for riding Silas so well. And now tea, I think, don't you?'

14

'We'll go up the main drive,' I said, 'now that I know the way. Then we won't have to unwire gates. I cut my hands last time, but none of you noticed because you were so wrapped up in Melody and her dear little freak.'

'Poor Lynne! Still, you were spared the disgrace of a search party.'

'Supposing Fred is there?'

'We'll tell him the truth, which is what you should have done in the beginning.'

'He was so angry and I felt such a fool locking myself in. I only wanted to creep away and hide.'

'The more idiotic you've been, the more important it is to put on a brave face,' suggested David, who is really rather mature for his twelve years. 'And you won't make a vet if you're timid. Vets have to be decisive,' he added, standing on his pedals to make his bicycle go faster up the hill.

When we reached the house with its tall chimneys and overgrown garden we were surprised to find that the grass had been cut and some of the hedges trimmed.

'Perhaps the owner is coming back from abroad like Rochester in *Jane Eyre*,' I suggested. 'Perhaps it will be done up and made beautiful again for a house party.'

'We musn't romanticize. This is a business project. We must keep our heads and exercise self-control.'

'You sound like Mirabelle,' I said. 'This way.'

We dismounted, walked under the archway, with its crumbling little tower where the clock had been, and pushed our way through an army of willowherb.

'Where are the stables?' my brother's voice was incredulous.

'This way. Look, there!'

'Oh, really, I don't think they'll do, do you? They're so dreadfully overgrown. Just think of the other place – automatic drinking bowls, electricity laid on, purpose-built, modern, clean and hygienic.'

'But if we cut down that elder tree and clear the weeds. . . . Come and look inside. See how good the bricks are. These were fine stables for carriage horses and hunters in their time.'

'Yes, in their time, but not now.'

'There are cobbles under these weeds,' I continued, 'and a brick apron, and the drainage is good. I checked that.'

'Choked,' said David.

'But clearable.'

'Maybe.'

'All the same this yard has possibilities if the other place falls through. Look,' I insisted, 'there's a pump I never saw last time. I wonder if it works.'

'How do we find out who the owners are?' David peeped into the tack room.

'I expect Fred would know. I say, look at these ventilators, and see how useful the loft is – there's a sort of chute for the hay to slide down.'

'I don't suppose modern lorry drivers like lofts,' observed David drily.

'Oh, you've got no imagination,' I cried.

'And you have too much,' he retorted.

'Take care going into the tack room. Remember what happened to me. The handle's broken,' I warned him.

'But it isn't. It's been mended.'

'Someone's been around then,' I said, mystified. 'Not Fred, surely. Why should he keep the place up?'

'Let's look a bit further,' David pushed his way through some briars and slipped round behind the stable block.

'I say, there's an isolation box here. How very useful,' he called. 'All bedded down, too.'

'You're joking,' I cried.

But he wasn't. A moment later I came upon him stroking a dun with black points and a black stripe down his back – a hardy-looking pony with large, strong hoofs.

'What are you doing here? I've told you before, the place is private. You've no business here. Can't you read?' With a leap of my heart I recognized Fred's voice and the next minute he was pushing us out of the way, his face the colour of crushed strawberries, his eyes very bright like flames from a Bunsen burner.

'Nosing around,' said David without shame.

'Trespassing,' retorted Fred.

'Is this a secret pony?' I asked, feeling brave now that David was there to support me.

Fred turned and spat into the bushes. 'None of your business. Go home and keep your traps shut,' he said.

'Please can you tell us one thing?' asked David. 'Who owns this place?'

'That little youngster was going for meat, off to the slaughter house and then over the water, so I bought him, bought him at the Fair where young Briony bought the mule what nobody wants. Mine's the best buy.'

'Actually the mule's already found a home,' I said rather smugly. 'He's going to be much admired, a favourite exhibit for years and years. But we're so pleased that you've saved this little pony. How very kind of you. And isn't he beautiful? Really sound and a very hardy type.'

'If by any chance Briony rents this place, I'm sure she'll be happy for this pony to stay,' David put in.

A silence fell then and I could almost feel Fred adjusting to the new situation. I made a face at David, demonstrating that I thought he had made a false move, for how could Briony bear to have Fred around all the time? But David was not to be dissuaded. 'After all, you saved our foal's life,' he added, 'and we're all good friends.'

'She gave me the hunting horn for that. I've got it here. What about a blast?'

Fred was running away from the question David had put, and suddenly I think we both realized that he had never quite matured, perhaps partly because he had never known his parents, having grown up in an orphanage.

'Just a soft one, not too loud. We don't want to bring round the nosey parkers buzzing like a lot of bees turned out of their hive.' He tooted a few times, telling us what the noises meant, and then he told us that the place was coming up for sale in a few days' time. The owner had died a year ago, but there had been a dispute over his will, so the place had stood empty. He was an old man who had let it go to ruin because he had no children to inherit it. Fred thought that the stables might eventually be converted into cottages because they were soundly built of stone. The house had seen better days but could be restored.

'It might make a fine place for young Briony if she would get a bit more sense into her head. There's running water and a good floor under here,' Fred kicked at the weeds with a boot. 'And a couple of paddocks and a spinney for shelter.'

'I doubt she could take on such a tumbledown place,' David admitted.

'Well, I've said my piece,' Fred told us. 'Now go home quietly if you don't mind. I don't want this pony discovered. I'll move him in a couple of days. I've got a shed up at the end of my garden all nice and ready. I haven't done anyone any harm and I've done this little fellow a power of good.'

'We're so grateful to you . . .' I began, only to be slapped down by Fred's gruff 'We don't want any soft-soaping here. I think we understand each other well enough now.'

'Yes, yes,' agreed David quickly. 'Thanks for the information. Let's go, Lynne. Good luck with the pony!'

'And not a word to anyone, mind!' shouted Fred. 'Mum's the word, and don't you forget. You broke your promise last time, Lynne.'

'What an evening!' sighed David as we pedalled away. 'He *was* in a tizzy. Well, we'd better find out more about the place, just in case, but I don't see how Briony can afford to put it in working order.'

'It's only a tiny possibility,' I said, 'just a little dream.'

'That modern yard is a hundred times better,' David said.

15

Sunday passed uneventfully, apart from a freak thunderstorm. Briony delivered Silas to the two girls who wanted to try him for the Prince Philip Cup. David and I struggled with our homework and visited the mares and their foals. Melody and her mule were to leave for the farm park in a couple of days, where they were to have a small paddock of their own next to the oxen. Briony had called the mule Sherpa, because his species are useful on mountain paths, and Candy's foal Stowaway, remarking that nobody had known he was on the boat when Candy left Ireland.

David described the stables at Lambswood Manor to Briony and our parents, who baulked at the idea of taking on a place in need of so much repair. In any case, our sister had set her heart on the other yard, even though it was three miles away. But on Monday she learned that the rent being asked was much more than she could afford. The estate agents could not recommend a reduction because a polo club had shown an interest and, having a very rich membership, could probably afford the asking price.

Briony was sunk in gloom. 'I'm very sorry, but you may just have to put up with Candy being sold,' she told me. 'Even if we have stables I may be tempted to sell her if the right buyer turns up. You must simply harden your heart.'

'She seems so absolutely right for me,' I insisted. 'She's fifteen hands, so I'll never grow out of her, she's four, so she'll last me twenty years – perhaps – and we like each other.'

'Yes, I see. But on the other hand, fifteen hands is an awkward size. Most classes are for ponies under fourteen two hands high. She hasn't got a pedigree so you can't show her as a Connemara. She's too small to be a good working hunter or a top jumper and too big to be in any pony classes. And she hasn't quite enough thoroughbred blood to be a small hack.'

'But I don't mind about not competing. I'll jump her for pleasure, not for gain or applause. If I'm going to be a vet, I shan't have the time to be a top rider as you were.'

Meanwhile Dad suddenly seemed more cheerful and talked airily of a business trip to the Middle East. 'I can always help you out if you get absolutely stuck,' he told Briony to our astonishment.

The secretary had taken to the hollow-backed bay mare and on Monday, after school, Briony hurried us to our nearest field to see a new purchase – a lean mare with beautiful limbs who grazed fitfully.

'She's highly strung but with tremendous potential. I'm going to train her,' Briony said, the gloom lifting at last, 'and then sell her in October. I bought her from a young man who used to do a lot of pony-clubbing and now wants to train jumpers. She's a bit small for his purposes. He bought her on impulse. You see, I'm not the only one to do that. And I don't have to pay him until I've found her a home.'

'What's his name?'

'Why, Lynne?'

'I just wondered.'

'Mervyn Fairfax.'

'Nice.'

'Nice what?'

'Name.'

'Not nice, nice is an awful word,' Briony said.

'I'm going to see Candy,' I said, jogging away down the lane, partly because escape from school always made me want to run.

I called, and Candy came at the canter with Stowaway trotting behind. Then I thought for the hundredth time how awful it would be if Briony couldn't rent stables and Candy was sold, and I had to push away from myself an intense and sudden jealousy as Mirabelle went riding by on her chestnut, Mercury. She waved and I waved back and then deliberately turned away, not trusting myself to speak.

Stowaway seemed much taller now, because his legs had straightened and lost the spiderish look which I had noticed when he was first born. In fact I could not now understand how he had managed to fit inside his mother – he seemed so large and angular. How could he have folded up so neatly? He was very friendly but Sherpa kept his distance, both reflecting, perhaps, their mothers' attitudes to the human race.

'Tomorrow you're going on a journey,' I told Sherpa. 'It's all fixed up at last and you musn't be frightened because Briony drives very well and corners very slowly. Nothing awful will happen and you'll arrive in a lovely park with lots of fields. Hundreds of people will come specially to see you. You're going to be a celebrity. Mules are a dying race in this country and loads of little children will long to stroke your muzzle.'

He looked at me with his small dark eyes encircled by donkey make-up, his mealy nose twitching. Then Candy butted me gently for attention, her head now definitely more golden than cream in its summer coat, her body looking trim and well put-together. I imagined myself teaching her to jump. Would she be any good? 'Yes,' a voice inside me replied. 'All Irish ponies jump – it's in their blood.'

I turned the future over in my mind like someone turning over soil in the hope of finding a gold coin. 'If only The Mountain were a mare he could breed a foal and be useful,' I mused, patting Candy's neck as she stood beside me like a faithful dog. 'But Briony was given him on condition that she kept him for ever and ever. Nobody could possibly know that he was going to suffer from chronic lameness.' As I spoke I knew that in my heart I was resenting The Mountain a little because he would be occupying one of the two looseboxes in the winter, and I knew that my resentment was wrong and unfair.

Presently I walked back to the house and, after finishing my homework and watching a television programme, I went to bed. I dreamt that Fred had set the tumbledown stables on fire. The flames turned the night sky into an inferno of red and gold, and I woke with the smell of burning wood still in my nose. Being superstitious, I sprang from my bed, went to the window and looked out to see that the sky had become a golden sea streaked with red. Remembering how my premonition had been right about Candy's difficulties, I dressed and went outside only to find that the red had become a rose pink and the gold the fragile light of dawn tinged with pale apricot. My dream had become more real than reality, distorting truth. Was I too fanciful to become a vet?

'Checking the foals? They're all right. I've just visited them,' Fred said.

'Oh, you made me jump. It's kind of you to keep an eye on them for us. Thank you very much. I had a nightmare. I dreamt the Lambswood stables were on fire,' I shivered at the memory. 'I hope it's not a bad omen.'

'Still interested in them, are you?'

'Oh yes, but even if they are available, they'll probably be too expensive for Briony to rent.'

'I should ask young Mirabelle,' suggested Fred, who was really at his best in the early morning. 'She's a daft girl, too fat to be a good rider, but she might be able to help you.'

'How do you mean?'

'Well, she's got a rich dad, hasn't she? Stacks of money. Ask her and see. Those who don't ask, don't get.'

The old look of irritation returned to Fred's eyes and then, to my horror, he took the hunting horn from between the second and third buttons of his jacket and blew a resounding 'Goneaway!'

'Tally ho!' he shouted.

'Oh, no!' I cried.

'It's time folks were awake, the lazy devils. It's past dawn; it's sunrise,' Fred gave his loud scornful laugh. 'The early bird catches the early work. I've mucked my little pony out already. He's coming on a treat. Want to have a go?' He handed me the horn.

'No thanks!'

'Are you scared then? Think I have some disease?' He sounded angry.

'No. I'm afraid I won't be able to blow hard enough.'

'Those who don't try, don't get.'

'Mother will be annoyed. She sleeps late. I'm off now,' I started jogging down the lane, followed by the sound of Fred's voice singing 'D'ye Ken John Peel?'

16

'I may keep the new mare a little longer,' Briony announced. 'If I sell her in October I might get a thousand pounds, but if I wait until the spring I'll get much more. I've called her Coriander, by the way.'

I said nothing. What could I say? Those words seemed to seal Candy's fate. The Mountain and Coriander would each have a loosebox.

'Could Mervyn Fairfax supply stabling for her?' I suggested at last. 'Then you could still do a little agency work.'

'But he's short himself. That's one of the reasons why he unloaded Coriander on to me,' Briony said. 'I'm gradually coming round to the idea of closing down for the winter, selling off all the stock, and taking a secretarial course. I'll get up early, ride Coriander before I go to work until it gets too dark, and then just at weekends until March.'

'Most secretarial courses aren't absolutely full-time,' Mother said. 'If you go to the college I'm thinking about, some mornings you won't have to be in until ten o'clock.'

I turned away, for I could think of no argument which would convince either my mother or Briony that Candy rather than Coriander should have the spare loosebox, because riding was my sister's job, whereas with me it was simply a hobby.

'Oh, for heaven's sake, don't look so down-in-the-mouth,' Briony cried. 'Candy's not the only lovable pony in the world. There'll be others and riding in the winter isn't such fun anyway.'

'Things are picking up,' Mother said. 'Business is better. I'll start earning soon, so next year matters will improve. Darling, if you were going to make a career out of riding, we should raise heaven and hell to get you a pony, but you'll be working for your O Levels and then your A Levels. Lots and lots of girls are in your situation, wanting ponies and not being able to have them.'

'But I've got one,' I insisted. 'I feel as if Candy is mine already. I know I haven't bought her, but I've nursed her. I've grown fond of her, don't you see?'

'Yes, of course, we see, but ponies are ponies. If you grow fond of one you can easily grow fond of another. After all, you loved Nugget, but in the end you managed to part with him.'

'That was different. He was outgrown – we couldn't ride him any more, could we? And he was bored.'

'Look, we can go on arguing for ages and it won't get us anywhere,' Briony said. 'Nothing's definite. Perhaps some stabling will turn up. I'm still asking around.'

'There's Lambswood Manor,' I said. 'David and I looked at the stabling. Don't you remember? We told you.'

'Yes, and I've found out the name of the agent handling the property. I'll ring now, but I haven't much hope, Lynne. I haven't enough money to rebuild tumbledown stables.'

'She allows herself to be driven by circumstances,' my mother remarked as Briony went to the phone. 'She's become very fatalistic since the death of Talisman. Have you noticed? She's not really making much effort to find stabling. She thinks fate will decide.'

'Nothing venture, nothing win,' I quoted.

'That's my view too,' Mother said, 'but remember Briony has had three setbacks in a row. The Mountain

103

going lame and her boyfriend giving her up as well as Talisman's sudden end. It's a lot to take in a matter of six months. I wish she'd throw over the agency and go back to show-jumping or three-day eventing, because I think she has terrific talent as a rider, but I appreciate her reasons for stopping. I would have done the same in the circumstances.'

'Oh, but I love the agency. I love having so many ponies passing through. I think it's tremendous fun. Something's always happening. If I hadn't become fond of Candy I should be perfectly happy.'

'No luck,' Briony reappeared. 'The place has been sold, stables and all, subject to contract, of course, but the agents say it seems straightforward. All the surveys have been done.'

I looked out of the window at rainwashed skies. My heart felt heavy; a little nagging ache started between my eyebrows. In my mind a fantasy began a slow death. There seemed nothing to look forward to. Stowaway would grow and then leave for the farm park, and then someone would come with a cheque book and buy Candy and she would disappear out of my life. In the spring there would be other ponies to ride, but they wouldn't be Candy.

'I can pay you back the money I owe you for your share of Nugget,' Briony said. 'In fact, I must.'

'Thanks.' My voice was leaden, for that sum wasn't enough to pay half the cost of Candy.

'When you're a vet you'll be able to buy yourself all the ponies you want. Vets can earn such a lot,' Mother said.

'Yes, and I'll have a dog too. At last!'

I stormed out of the room, for, suddenly, life seemed utterly unfair.

'It's not as though we bought Briony her horses. I mean, she earned them . . .' Mother's voice followed me, maddening in its logic. My sister had been lucky – the sort of rider who is naturally lent horses. The Mountain had become hers when his owner had gone abroad and wanted a good home for him and after Talisman's death, other people had offered to lend her mounts but, grief-stricken, she had refused them all. On the other hand nobody had ever asked me to ride their animal in a show, apart from Briony. I simply wasn't outstanding like her.

Melody and Sherpa had gone to the farm park, but I walked down the lane to talk to Candy and Stowaway and on the way I met Mirabelle on her chestnut, Mercury.

'Heavens, has something happened? You look dreadful!' Her blue eyes were shiny with concern, like stones washed by the sea. I looked at her anxious face, my envy battling with a feeling of friendship. She really sounded as though she cared. 'Is Candy all right?'

'Until she's sold. I don't want her to go, Mirabelle! I thought we might get Lambswood Manor stables. I built a dream round them, and now I know they're sold and there's no hope.'

'Oh,' said Mirabelle, looking surprised. 'Oh, I see. Lambswood seems to ring a bell, a very loud bell. Perhaps something can be done. I don't know. I'll speak to Daddy. He's a very powerful person.'

'I'm sure he is, thank you,' I said.

I continued to the field and Mirabelle called over the fence, 'Something may turn up. I shouldn't give up hope.'

Candy and Stowaway came and stood with me, as though they liked my company, and my happiness at their affection was tinged with sorrow at the thought of losing them. Suddenly I was full of self-pity and renewed envy. Why should Mirabelle have two ponies and me none? It simply wasn't fair, I decided for the hundredth time. And yet at the back of my mind there was also the feeling that I wasn't really a very nice person, for I had spurned Mirabelle's concern and turned my back on her offer to speak to her father, which was probably well meant. 'I'm a beastly person,' I told Candy, 'eaten up by envy and disappointment. I don't suppose I deserve to succeed.'

Then I saw a fat woman beckoning me from over the gate. I walked back.

'Yes, can I help?'

'The cream mare, is she for sale?'

Pale eyes, neither blue nor grey, seemed to search my face; podgy hands pounded the air as though attempting to emphasize the importance of the question.

'Why, do you want to buy her?' My voice was calm, but inside my stomach had turned over and a sudden weakness had drained my legs of power.

'It's possible. Does she belong to Briony Fletcher?' There was something about the woman's nose that reminded me of a hippopotamus.

'Yes, I'm afraid she does.'

'Why afraid?'

'Oh, I can't explain. I'm sorry. It's a long story.'

'Is she quiet to ride?'

'Not really. I mean she hasn't been schooled.'

'She's very pretty. Would she carry me, do you suppose?'

I looked at my questioner carefully as though assessing her, although I already knew my answer.

'Or am I too heavy?'

'I'm afraid you are, definitely. You need a cobbier animal, a Fell pony or a cob of fifteen two.' Relief made me sound merry – I knew Briony would have felt the same way, so I was letting nobody down.

'My niece,' the woman said. 'She might do for my niece.'

'Look,' I suggested on a sudden wave of inspiration, 'write down your telephone number and I'll talk to my sister. The mare's not available until the foal is weaned in January, and then she'll need schooling.'

'My name's Hodges, Miss Felicity Hodges. There – rather a scruffy old envelope, I'm afraid, but legible.'

'Thanks, I'll pass it on. But don't expect to hear for several months.'

'No, but she's a dream pony, no mistake about that.'

'Yes, I know,' I said, pushing the address into my pocket, my heart diving into my training boots.

When I handed the envelope to Briony, she said she would file it just in case. 'I've no idea what our situation will be next January. We might be desperate for a home for Candy. One just never knows.' And her words lodged in the back of my mind – a little threat which came out in the middle of the night like a mouse to nibble at any optimism that I might feel. Yet all the time, unknown to me, new forces were at work. Help was to come from a most unlikely source and we were all to feel a little ashamed of jealousies we had harboured against the bearer of the news. Perhaps we had under-estimated Briony's charm and attraction as a well known rider.

It was the first day of the summer holidays when Mirabelle turned up on our front doorstep with a wide smile of triumph on her freckled face.

'Can I see Briony?'

'Of course. She's just put the kettle on for coffee. Do you want any?' asked David.

'Not really, thank you. I just want to talk.'

She came inside with her black labrador, Percy, at her heels.

'Hullo, school problems? Mercury throwing up her head again?' asked Briony, looking dashing in nylon breeches and a quilted waistcoat, for the day was cold for July.

'No, no problems. Everything's great.'

Once again Mirabelle's face reminded me of a tomato splitting in the sun, her smile was so wide and her cheeks rosy from fresh air and sunlight, for her skin never tanned.

'Lynne mentioned your interest in Lambswood,' she began.

'Not mine, really. I've never been there. To be honest, it sounds too tumbledown for someone without any capital.'

'Only we're going to own it!' Mirabelle announced.

'Not really!'

For a terrible moment my jealousy seemed unbounded. She was even to have the place I loved! This was too much. My whole body tingled with envy.

'Lucky you. Will you do the place up?' asked Briony.

'Yes. But I only have two ponies, so Dad thought you might like to use the rest. I mean, would that solve your problems? We'd love you to be there. Dad's going to install a swimming pool too.'

'I haven't seen the place,' Briony began cautiously, 'but it sounds a wonderful offer. I should want to pay rent, of course.'

'Well, not very much, because Dad says it will be great to have you around. Your horses will impress his overseas customers. He's going to make the whole place very posh. He entertains a lot of Arabs and they love horses, of course. He's going to be away a lot too, with Mummy, so he'd like to feel you'll be there to pick me up if I fall off. Candy can have a stable next to Mercury.'

'It's terribly kind of you, but listen, I can only consider a proper business proposition,' said Briony.

'Yes, well, Dad says you're to make an appointment to see him, through his secretary. Is that businesslike enough?'

'Yes, yes, that's fine. Let's take the truck now and visit the place. Can we? Would your father mind?' Briony suddenly sounded eager.

'No, of course not. But why not walk? Wouldn't that save money?'

'She's right,' David said. 'Mirabelle has inherited business sense.'

'Well, time can be money, but not now,' Briony said.

Ten minutes later we were in the yard, which had been partly cleared of weeds.

'The tack room has a sink and a fireplace and super panelling,' Mirabelle told us. 'But the stalls must be turned into looseboxes. There's even an isolation box round the back where you can quarantine your horses from Ireland.'

'It's very sheltered, and I love the clock tower,' Briony said.

'Oh, Dad's going to have that restored. He says it's a prestige building. He's going to restore the whole place. And David, you can ride Venus if you like.'

'Thanks, but I hope eventually to have a pony of my own.'

'I was just thinking you might improve her. You know she shies a lot, through naughtiness rather than fear. And, Briony, Dad really is over the moon about the possibility that you may take the place. He admires you so much as a rider. He says you have star quality. You'll be a business asset.'

'I find that hard to believe,' Briony laughed.

'But things are picking up for you, aren't they?' said Mirabelle.

'Not really. I don't know what you mean,' our sister sounded incredulous.

'Your father. His business is picking up, isn't it?'

109

'No, not as far as we know,' Briony said. 'He's been hit by inflation.'

'But he's won a contract in the Middle East. Hasn't he told you? Not much, but a start. Dad knows, because one of his smaller companies was competing for it too. Your father offered better delivery dates and after-purchase servicing, or whatever it's called.'

'It's news to us, although I must admit Dad's been looking more cheerful lately,' David said. 'Mirabelle, you certainly keep your ear to the ground!'

'I expect your father's waiting until it's all signed and sealed.'

'Yes, maybe,' Briony agreed.

'There are two paddocks and a spinney and one pony shelter,' Mirabelle told us. 'And a large meadow the other side of the house. I'm going to have a huge bedroom with three windows. I shan't know myself with a private bathroom!'

'Let's go back and I'll ring your father's secretary,' Briony suggested. 'I really am enthusiastic, so long as it's a business proposition.'

'Yes, come on. I can't wait for it all to happen,' Mirabelle said. 'I've been so bored on my own. It's terrible being an only child – you've no idea. Especially when Mum and Dad are away so much. I don't know how I would have survived without all of you just up the road.'

17

Several days later, Mother said, 'You know sometimes if you keep on trying hard enough things suddenly get offered to you on a plate, but I'm convinced this wouldn't happen if you hadn't slogged away first. It's a sort of Divine Providence.'

'I'm sure you're right,' Briony said. 'I'm going to discuss modernization and alterations with the architect tomorrow, and Mervyn Fairfax is going to give me some advice. Mirabelle's father has been working away quietly behind the scenes so that when the will was settled he could come in right away with an offer, having had all the surveys completed and everything.'

'And as for you and Dad,' David said ruefully, 'why didn't you tell us your good news? We didn't expect to hear it from Mirabelle.'

'I didn't want to raise your hopes until it was definite. Anyway, it's only a beginning, something to build on, but if Lynne really wants Candy, and David finds a pony to his taste, I daresay we'll be able to help out presently. Give us a few more weeks until all the contracts are signed and then, so long as the work force doesn't strike, we might be able to help a bit financially.'

'Thank you, thank you very much. The terrible thing about being a vet is the thought that I shan't actually be earning anything for years and years,' I said.

'All the greatest achievements take time,' Mother observed.

'A yard,' I mused. 'A yard with a clock tower and a

111

panelled tack room, and horses' heads looking out! Doesn't it seem like a dream come true?'

'Sort of,' said Briony, 'but we'll move slowly.'

'Not if the whole enterprise is to be used partly as a promotional asset for Mirabelle's father's company,' Dad said. 'He'll want it to appear successful. You'll have a telephone laid on and running water and all that.'

'I'm not sure I deserve it,' Briony said.

'Oh yes you do. It's time you had some good luck,' cried Mother. 'I'm so delighted for you.'

I left them to see Candy. 'You're staying,' I told her, 'and everything's going to get better and better. In the early spring I'll start to school you. Mother and Dad will have more money so you should enjoy plenty of oats and pony cubes. There'll be a loosebox looking out on a cobbled yard towards a house with tall chimneys, where you will sleep on winter nights, and a paddock for daytime. We must never despair, Candy, because we never know what good luck is waiting for us round the corner. I've wasted so much energy worrying about your future when all the time everything was going to turn out all right in the end.'

As I spoke, Stowaway started to pull at my coat, clasping it between his pink gums.

'And we'll do our best for you too,' I said. 'Oh yes, I promise we'll eventually find you a good and loving home.'

Now the golden sunshine was warm on my back; the sweet smells of high summer scented the balmy air as my optimism ran ahead of me into the future like a messenger bearing good news. I felt suddenly as though nothing could ever go wrong again.